Gregory Hill

Nice Guys Don't Always Finish Last

Gregory Hill

Nice Guys Don't Always Finish Last

A comic twist on a young boys school years

JustFiction Edition

Impressum/Imprint (nur für Deutschland/only for Germany)
Bibliografische Information der Deutschen Nationalbibliothek: Die Deutsche Nationalbibliothek verzeichnet diese Publikation in der Deutschen Nationalbibliografie; detaillierte bibliografische Daten sind im Internet über http://dnb.d-nb.de abrufbar.
Alle in diesem Buch genannten Marken und Produktnamen unterliegen warenzeichen-, marken- oder patentrechtlichem Schutz bzw. sind Warenzeichen oder eingetragene Warenzeichen der jeweiligen Inhaber. Die Wiedergabe von Marken, Produktnamen, Gebrauchsnamen, Handelsnamen, Warenbezeichnungen u.s.w. in diesem Werk berechtigt auch ohne besondere Kennzeichnung nicht zu der Annahme, dass solche Namen im Sinne der Warenzeichen- und Markenschutzgesetzgebung als frei zu betrachten wären und daher von jedermann benutzt werden dürften.

Coverbild: www.ingimage.com

Verlag: JustFiction! Edition ist ein Imprint der
LAP LAMBERT Academic Publishing GmbH & Co. KG
Heinrich-Böcking-Str. 6-8, 66121 Saarbrücken, Deutschland
Telefon +49 681 37 20 310, Telefax +49 681 37 20 310-9
Email: info@justfiction-edition.com

Herstellung in Deutschland:
Schaltungsdienst Lange o.H.G., Berlin
Books on Demand GmbH, Norderstedt
Reha GmbH, Saarbrücken
Amazon Distribution GmbH, Leipzig
ISBN: 978-3-8454-4541-0

Imprint (only for USA, GB)
Bibliographic information published by the Deutsche Nationalbibliothek: The Deutsche Nationalbibliothek lists this publication in the Deutsche Nationalbibliografie; detailed bibliographic data are available in the Internet at http://dnb.d-nb.de.
Any brand names and product names mentioned in this book are subject to trademark, brand or patent protection and are trademarks or registered trademarks of their respective holders. The use of brand names, product names, common names, trade names, product descriptions etc. even without a particular marking in this works is in no way to be construed to mean that such names may be regarded as unrestricted in respect of trademark and brand protection legislation and could thus be used by anyone.

Cover image: www.ingimage.com

Publisher: JustFiction! Edition
is an imprint of the publishing house
LAP LAMBERT Academic Publishing GmbH & Co. KG
Heinrich-Böcking-Str. 6-8, 66121 Saarbrücken, Germany
Phone +49 681 37 20 310, Fax +49 681 37 20 310-9
Email: info@justfiction-edition.com

Printed in the U.S.A.
Printed in the U.K. by (see last page)
ISBN: 978-3-8454-4541-0

Nice Guys Don't Always Finish Last

By Gregory Hill

I dedicate this book to my mother, Jane Hill. She has looked after me my entire life and like most mums she has done so with seemingly little appreciation from me and my two siblings. This is my way of saying thank you for twenty years of cleaning up after me, driving me to places and putting up with my idiocy. Thanks Mum

Chapter 1 - Birthday Surprises

Now before I start the story there is a few things you should know about me. I'm 14 years old, my name is Martin Hill, and I live a town called Bracknell that's over run with chavs and pregnant teenagers. I kinda stick out in a crowd since I'm six foot three inches, I have brown hair and grey eyes and what many would call a "strange sense of humour". My girlfriend is called Jade Barthel and she plays a big part in the story. Oh and one more thing about me, even if I don't seem it all the time in the story I am actually "too nice for my own good" as my family put it but that's because I like to help people. Well anyway here's the story.

It was a normal school day, well as normal as they get these days anyway. I got up, got dressed in the awful school uniform that was forced upon us (shirt, tie and an awful maroon V-neck jumper), tried to skip all the stairs and nearly broke my ankle and cracking my skull open (and that's if I did it right!). I said hi to my mum and my sister then made my lunch and got out of the house as quick as I could.

I know it might seem a bit strange that I want to get to school but I had a good reason and no it wasn't because I was sad or a geek (although I do have my geeky tendencies just like everyone else). It was my girlfriend's birthday and I had to play a practical joke on her on the way into school, you know as you do to the person you love. Me and my friend Andrew were going to meet by the bike sheds at school so we can prepare the joke.

As usual, Andrew was late, but I knew he would be so I told him to meet me half an hour earlier than when I was going to turn up. If he turned up on time then it'll get him back for all the times he's been late before so it's a win, win situation. I told him to turn up at seven but he turned up at twenty-five-to-eight so I wasn't far out.

Anyway, where was I? Oh yeah, the joke! Well first he said 'Hi Martin' and I said 'Hi Andy' and then I had to remind him what the plan was, he's forgetful like that. He liked to blame this on the fact that if it wasn't for school he wouldn't wake up until four in the afternoon (I have actually woken him up at four PM before so don't think it's just me exaggerating) but anyone who knows Andy can confirm that his brain works at the rate of one thought an hour. So after I told him the plan for the eighth time I got my water pistol out my bag and handed it to Andy, he then ran and hid up the tree over the cycle path. I then got the squirty cream out of my bag and hid round the corner in another tree.

Now before I go any further, the idea here was for Andy to soak Jade and then for me to squirt the cream on her (yeah I know the dirty minded among you are sniggering at that... as am I, ha-ha), the result, as you can imagine, didn't go to well for Andy and me. He missed with the water pistol and got Jade's sister instead of Jade, Hayley slapped him round the face for getting her new shirt wet and making it see through (Andy didn't mind that bit too much though, "small price to pay mate" he whispered to me with a huge grin on his face). When I tried to get Jade with the cream it missed and got Hayley in the face so it looked like... well you can imagine what it looked like, so I got a couple of slaps for that but I made Jade laugh immensely so I guess it wasn't too bad.

Afterwards we walked with Jade and Hayley back to school discussing how every year we tried and failed to play a practical joke on Jade.

'I dunno, last year was pretty good, we did manage to make you fall off your bike and hurt your knee' Andy was just saying.

'Yes but we were trying to make her go into the bucket of glue and the feathers,' I just cracked up laughing at that point as I remembered what happened, 'then you were so angry it didn't work you ran at her and you got the glue and feathers!'

'Yeah I still hate you guys for that one, I couldn't do sports day because of that!' Jade said as she always does whenever this subject comes up, which is quite a lot because we like embarrassing Jade to see the look on her face. It's probably our favourite pass time but don't worry, she gives as good as she gets.

But I was ready to calm her down again this time 'But you love me really?' I said sweetly, which, me being 6 foot 3, just made me seem weird.

'Yeah... but... I can't help that!' Jade spluttered after thinking about it for a while. She was the most beautiful girl in the world with her long blonde hair and her bluey green eyes that you could just get lost in for hours at a time... but she wasn't... the sharpest tool in the shed. She was really smart and everything but she was really, really slow... and blind, not literally blind but you know what I mean.

'Hmmm... should I let you have your present after that remark?' I said and she did the predictable Jade thing to do afterwards.

She turned suddenly hyper jumping round and round in circles yelling 'Presents! Presents!' one of the things that defines Jade's behaviour is how she can instantly change from tired or moody to hyper, it was like flicking a switch. It didn't even take much to set her off; her "inner child" was very much in control of her.

After she calmed down she put on her puppy dog look and asked me really sweetly (much better than I did) 'Can I have my pwesent now? Pwease?'

'What's in it for me?' I asked, I could have just given it to her and lived up to my reputation of being the "Nice Guy" but let's be honest, being evil is also really fun.

'Ummmmmmm... my love for ever and ever?' she said clearly thinking hard. At this point Hayley and Andy stopped listening and turned away embarrassed, well actually they lasted longer than I thought they would.

'Don't I have that already?' I replied with a mock-astonished look on my face. OK now I'm really disproving the "Nice Guy" thing, making a girl wait for her birthday present (from their point of view at least) is tantamount to stealing or murder, but honestly I am nice

'Well... yeah... but...' she stuttered.

'Oh for Christ's sake, just give it to her Martin we're nearly at school and we do not want her to embarrass us anymore by her being... well Jade!' Andy said afraid of making his reputation worse, which I thought was impossible but at Brakenhale School you never know.

'Fine! Spoil my fun why don't you!' I said taking a well wrapped, by my sister, present out of my pocket and gave it to her.

Her face lit up at the sight of the present, while she was ripping of the wrapping paper Andy said 'your present from me is... err... in the shops, still but you probably expected that.' However, Jade was not paying him any attention; she had just taken the silver necklace I bought her out of the box. It was a silver outline of a heart on a silver chain. Simple but elegant, just the way she liked her jewellery

'Wow!' that's apparently all she could say as she just kept staring at it not saying anything, the shape of her open mouth made a perfect circle. Then all of a sudden, there were two arms around my neck and she was kissing me repeatedly whilst hanging off me like my own swinging pendulum (yes I did just compare myself to a grandfather clock).

'Glad you like it' I said struggling to breathe and stay upright under the added weight.

Later that day I was going round her house for dinner with her family to celebrate the fact that she has survived another year in Bracknell without getting shot or stabbed or beaten up by the chavs. Jade warned me that her great uncles would be there and would constantly torment me but I said I could live with it, but I was starting to doubt that because she seemed to be trying to prepare me for it.

'Remember Dave? They constantly kept asking him why he liked me and giving him threats about what they would do if he hurt me. And you know what? When we broke up he ended up hanging upside down off a bridge over the motorway!' she said during maths the third lesson of the day.

'Yeah but I keep telling you I'm not letting you go without a fight' I said for the umpteenth time that morning 'and anyway they can't be that bad if they are related to you'

'I think you said that wrong, that's just more reason for them to be absolutely evil' said Jade finally admitting that she's evil which I had been saying for years.

Jade and me weren't always together, well... obviously, we actually got together a couple of weeks ago. But we had a bit of a head start seeing, as we were best mates for a year or two before. We ended up getting together two weeks ago, on a coach on the way back from a school trip. She asked one of her friends to find out if I liked her on the way to the trip a week before but I evaded the question. The thing is that whilst Jade only realised she liked me about three months ago, I realised I liked her about one month after we first met so for the last year and a half or more my feelings had just been growing and growing for her. I thought I was gunna be her best friend for the rest of my life never telling her how I felt but, apparently, she's a lot braver with that stuff than me and just told me. I still have the notebook in which she wrote the message saying she fancied me.

Anyway, where was I...? Oh yeah saying how Jade was being too paranoid. Well as the day went on I started to get a bit nervous, and all the stories and warnings from Jade weren't exactly helping. I didn't even notice the insults that were being hurled at me during tutor because I was so worried. I wasn't exactly in the popular group, as we said we were the outcast group, who all stick together because there's nobody else who would want us to stick with us. Although as the years pass we seem to be integrating more with the other groups, Rose used to be in the "popular kids" group but she comes and joins us at the hexagons more and more now. We even have a couple of friends from two years above us who come and join us and look out for us.

We rode to her house straight from school, and it was a funny journey because Jade forgets everything when she's riding her bike, it was quite a relief actually.

We got to her house and sat down in the lounge to watch blade trinity with Jade's dad. I liked him because he was funny, chilled out and trusts Jade not to do anything... too... explicit (that's the best way I could put it without being too crude). He was a very trusting person, very helpful and a laugh to be around. I couldn't see how Jades great uncles could be as bad as she says when they are related to her and her dad.

Still I was getting more and more nervous by the second! They were supposed to be there at six o'clock and before I knew it, it was five o'clock... half past... quarter too... five too... and then there was a knock at the door.

Me and Jade stood up and went to the door because she wanted to get the introductions over and done with as quick as possible. I however wasn't so keen to meet the dreaded great uncles.

Jade opened the door and there stood two people... both quite short... and one was a... a woman!

I was relieved to find out that this was her grandma and granddad and suddenly my stomach went back to normal, only to be replaced by more nervousness at the fact that they could turn up at any second.

There was another knock at the door two minutes later and I had the same feeling as I did last time... like the butterflies in my stomach were having a nuclear war inside me.

It turned out to be Jades Nan and other granddad. But they did come bearing good news... well good for me.

'Oh I nearly forgot, Dan and Steven aren't going to be able to come,' as soon as her Nan said this I was fighting the urge to jump up in the air and celebrate, 'yes it appears they have a business meeting at the office.'

'Really, what do they do?' I asked only just holding myself back from running up and giving her Nan a hug.

'Not much really, they just sit in an office and play solitaire on a computer' Jades granddad said.

When we were back in the lounge Jade gave me another bit of news… only not quite so good, 'You do know that Dan and Steven are my cousins?'

My happiness hit rock bottom again, at that moment I didn't like Jade as much as I did before. But then I looked at her and it was back to normal.

'Um… yeah of course I knew…'

'You didn't know did you?' she said

'No… no I didn't'

My pages must have been wide open at that point because even after all the warnings and the half dozen stories, she became very comforting.

'Don't worry; I'm sure they will like you. I mean the rest of my family do and that is pretty difficult.'

'Yeah but they don't hear all the sex jokes we make at school,' I said rather distraught.

'Yeah and neither will they… hopefully…' she replied making me feel slightly better and even smile a bit 'just be yourself and relax.' She's always been good at making me smile, even when we were just mates. She has always been there for me when I needed her the most, even if I wasn't planning on telling her what was wrong with me, she always managed to get it out of me… but now I think about most of the time that was helped by her nails…

'Yeah but it's the myself part of me that makes those jokes' I said

Her great uncles were next at the door; one of them was about six foot five and was taller than me, which didn't happen much as I'm six foot three (it's quite funny having all the teachers look up at you when they are telling you off). He was bald and looked like one of those bouncers who work at a clubs.

'These are my great uncles Kevin and-'

'Please don't say your Perry,' I burst out, I couldn't help myself.

Then all of a sudden the second great uncle started roaring with… well laughter actually.

'You wish mate! My names Damien,' he said shaking my hand rather vigorously, 'I take it your Martin. We've certainly heard a lot about you!'

'Really,' I said looking at Jade, 'well it's not true… unless it's good… then it is'

'Hahaha! Well I guess you are as funny as Jade tells us!' the first Uncle, Kevin said.

'Not in both meanings of the word I hope,' I was on a roll; I seem to have made a good impression with all of Jades family now. Maybe it's not going to be so bad after all…

'But,' Damien said suddenly ferocious and about half an inch away from my face, 'if you hurt her you'll end up like... that other one... what's his name... the one we locked in the freezer for a couple of hours?' he asked looking at Kevin.

'Mickey? Nick? David? Sam? Jamie?' Kevin replied looking puzzled.

'His name was Mike!' Jade said outraged.

'Yeah close enough,' Damien said 'anyways you'll end up like him but in more pain!' he finished dramatically.

'I would never hurt Jade because I love her!' I said angrily

'Yeah, yeah we've heard that one before. What makes you any different?' Kevin asked standing next to Damien and showing a height difference of about a foot.

'The fact that we were best friends before we got together and I don't need to try and find out what she likes and doesn't like. The fact that we understand how each other feel and the fact that unlike mike my love for her is one hundred percent pure,' Damien looked like he was about to interrupt at this point but I carried on 'so you can torment me all you want. You can hang me upside down off a bridge! You can push me down a flight of stairs! You can lock me up in a freezer for a week! I don't care because I'll survive it because I've I got Jade!'

They both looked stunned, so did Jade for that matter. We stood there for a moment or two. I was expecting a punch or to get thrown out of the house. But...

'Well this one has got a bit of flare in him!' Damien said laughing... but not at me... he was actually laughing with me!

'Yeah, I like him. He can stand up for himself and if he can do that he can stand up for Jade as well,' Kevin said patting me on the back.

'Let's keep him around for a while, see how he does and then we will see whether he gets our approval,' Damien said to Kevin who nodded.

The two brothers walked into the dining room to say hello to the other grown-ups while me and Jade walked back into the now empty lounge to watch the rest of the film.

'Did you mean that?' Jade asked after a few moments.

'Every word,' I said and she went bright red and just gave me a huge hug. Then we settled down to watch the rest of the movie. Don't you just love a soppy ending?

Chapter 2 - Glue And Feathers

The weekend after I was woken up by my alarm, you know one of those ones that carry on shouting at you until you throw it at the wall, yeah... there a huge crack in my wall now. Damn alarms. I normally turn mine off at the weekend but I forgot to on Friday... let's just say my mind was elsewhere and leave it at that.

I got down stairs in the normal fashion at the weekend, walking like a zombie and tripping halfway down. I got up from the floor and looked around. As usual there was my mum reading a book on the sofa and my sister was still in bed.

I made myself breakfast and sat down to watch TV and as usual there was nothing on, typical.

Then unusually considering it was before midday my mobile started ringing... and even more unusually it was my friend Charlie who has never woken up before four in the afternoon on a weekend.

'Yello?' I said, as I don't like saying a boring hello on the phone.

'Hey you finally awake then?' Charlie replied

'Finally? How long you been calling for then?'

'About an hour'

'Did you forget to turn off your alarm as well?'

'Yeah, man they are a pain in the ass! Anyway what was I about to say?' he asked. It really annoys me when people expect you to know what they are going to say before they have said it!

'Hold on I've got it written down here. How the hell am I supposed to know you idiot!'

'Just a figure of speech mate. God, calm down. Oh yeah I remember I was going to ask you whether you wanted to come out with me, Peter, Alida, William, Andy, Christine, Linda and Gareth... oh yeah, Jade's coming as well?' he asked

'What time?' I asked 'Where we going?'

'I dunno, just going to hang out I expect, maybe go to town, you can meet my girlfriend as well she's coming.' He replied

Well I couldn't pass down a chance to meet Charlie's new girlfriend could I? I mean it's a chance to embarrass him like hell... but wait... didn't he say Jade was going as well? Well that's a first! Charlie was smart for once! If I embarrassed him he would embarrass me... but... Jade already heard all the bad stories... what could he be planning? I thought.

So we were going to meet at the park near Charlie's house. Jade was already there by the time I got there, as I expected her to be, and so was Charlie. As I approached I got the feeling that they had hurriedly stopped their conversation as soon as they saw me, now I had reason to be suspicious if Jade was in on it as well. What could they be planning...?

'Hey there Martin,' Charlie said with a strange expression on his face... sort of like badly covered up excitement...

'Hi Martin,' Jade said with the same expression on her face.

'Hey,' I said after giving Jade a kiss 'what are you two up to?'

'I told you he would figure out what's happening; he's smarter than us and he can read you like a book' Charlie said accusingly to Jade.

'Well he might not have if you hadn't just said that! He'll just have to help us then won't he' Jade replied after a moment or two.

'Help you with what?' I asked

'Well we were planning on-'

'Shut up Andy's here!' Charlie said quietly interrupting Jade in mid-sentence.

'I'll tell you later' Jade whispered

Andy wasn't as awake as I was and didn't suspect anything, well actually he didn't look like he would react to an elephant running in front of him. He wasn't a morning person.

Over the next fifteen minutes the rest of them turned up and we started talking about school stuff and updating each other on all the gossip... actually that was just the girls the guys talked about games and the football match last week.

Without noticing it we sort of split into two sections as we walked, the guys lead the way towards town and the girls were behind talking about girly stuff that I would never understand even if I wanted to.

After ten or fifteen minutes there was an almighty great big noise coming from the girls... unless I was very much mistaken it was a huge chorus of 'awww's.

'What are they awwwing about back there?' Charlie asked me.

'Did you really say that Martin?' Alida asked me, now I knew what inspired those awwws.

'I know what it's about,' I said turning back to Charlie after nodding at Alida which caused more awwws, 'Jade just told them what I said to her uncles on her birthday' so I had to retell the story of Jades birthday to Charlie and the others.

'You actually shouted at them? Man... they got told!' said Peter after I finished the story. Peter was... well... vertically challenged is the nice way to put it, but I just say he's a midget.

'You're definitely one for the romantics aren't you Martin?' Charlie said to me. Charlie had been one of my best mates for years at this point but I still couldn't get how he could annoy me so much with simple things

'Well I wasn't going to stand there and be told I'm the same as David and Mike! The only way I was going to get their respect was to tell it to them straight and I wasn't going to risk losing Jade so I had to stand up to them' I said

'In your position mate I would have been kaking myself too much to say anything!' Peter said a look of awe on his face.

'Trust me; I needed to change boxers afterwards!' I said and everyone started laughing.

We had reached the town centre and the girls went one way while the guys went the other. I started walking with the guys towards the sports shop because we like going in there and loudly saying things about the clothes or all the chavs in there, but I was pulled back by the neck of my shirt. I turned around and saw Charlie pulling me back.

'Where do you think you're going? You're part of the plan now. We need to meet Jade and Alida in the alleyway behind burger king. Hurry up!' he said hurriedly

'Do you not think Peter might notice if Alida's gone? I mean he is her boyfriend' I said

'We'll deal with that when we have to but for now please hurry up before they see us' he said and we made a run for the alleyway.

When we got there Jade and Alida were already there. They were speaking quietly and I got snippets of their conversation before they saw us and stopped. All I managed to hear was '...not sure whether I like him anymore...'

That kind of scared me, but before I had time to think about what it meant she kissed me for a while, that kind of took my mind off it, if you know what I mean.

'Can you hurry this up a bit?' Charlie asked

I didn't stop kissing her I just stuck my middle finger up at him without looking; you see I have loads of talents that are useful... you just need the right situation to use them.

We broke apart then we started talking about the plan, which I didn't even know about.

'... And then Jade comes in and says-'Charlie was saying

'Wait, wait, wait. First of all what is the plan? You guys haven't told me yet!' I said a little annoyed.

'Charlie you said you would tell him on the way into town!' said Alida almost as annoyed as me. Alida was a nice girl, a really girly girl but yet again not too bright... It must be the blonde hair, I thought.

'I would have but the others were around us and we all got immersed in the story about Jades birthday and what Martin said!' Charlie replied just as angry.

'Hold it! Arguing isn't going to help and if we don't hurry up they will notice we've gone... that's if they haven't already.' Jade said stopping the argument and settling everything, she does that a lot 'we told the girls that we were going to go with you guys to another shop so we don't have much time.'

'Oops... that's what I forgot... I was supposed to come up with an excuse wasn't I?' Charlie said embarrassed.

'Charlie you-'

'Don't start this again!' Jade said to Alida before the argument could start 'Martin can go and keep Peter, Will and Andy distracted while we sort out the rest. Is that ok?' she asked turning to me

I mumbled an 'I guess' and I saw that as my cue to go and find the others.

I found Peter, Will and Andy in the sports shop still annoying the shop assistants.

'...And that one is far too bright and chavy... just like those guys over there' Peter was saying to a very old assistant who looked like he was in his seventies and about to hit him.

'Where have you been? We've been looking for you... where's Charlie?' Andy asked as soon as he saw me.

'Umm...' my mind was in overdrive trying to think of something 'he's... err... gone to ... go get his girlfriend!' my mind was brilliant, oh yeah, go me!

'So that's what they call it these days is it?' said Peter joining in the conversation.

I forced myself to laugh a bit but then I remembered what I had overheard the girls saying... '... Not sure whether I like him anymore'... that's what Jade had said... doesn't look too good for me I thought... but she had kissed me afterwards... or was that just an act? But she has said she loved me enough times... or was that an act as well?

I was so immersed in thought worrying about what it meant that I didn't notice a bucket of water being emptied on my head until the cold got through my hair (there was a lot of it).

'Hey! What the hell are you doing?' I shouted in rage at Will who was holding the now empty bucket

'You completely phased out on us, we had to check whether you were alive or not!' Peter explained

'Next time just poke me or check my pulse ok?' I said to them.

'What forced you into the pain of thought anyways?' Andy asked me

'It was definitely painful...' I muttered

'Didn't quite catch that' someone said but I was running the other way and didn't quite find out whom. I needed answers. If I learnt anything on Jades birthday it's to stand up for myself, even if I have to risk losing her. I'm not going to be messed around.

I ran to the centre of town and looked around. I saw Charlie running towards me.

'Where's Jade? I need to talk to her!' I said before he could ask what was wrong.

'She's in the game shop down the high street, if you're going to see her don't go in...' I didn't hear the rest I just sprinted towards the high street.

I got there and opened the door only to get another bucket of liquid on my head for the second time today. But this was different... this was sticky...

'What the-'before I could finish my sentence I got my body covered in feathers. Well the bottom half anyway

'Martin!' Jade shouted 'what are you doing here? Do you see why I said I don't like-'this was it I was going to hear it for myself '-Charlie anymore? He always gets it wrong and I ended up making my boyfriend look like a chicken instead of yours!' she finished saying to Alida.

'Why did you want to cover Peter in feathers?' I asked relieved but confused.

'Come on you can't say he hasn't told you?' Alida said angrily

'Told me what?' I asked now completely lost

'You honestly don't know?' Alida asked and I shook my head 'he's been cheating on me!'

'Wha-! That's ridic-! He loves you! What makes you think he's cheating on you?' I spluttered

'He has been going around town with this girl all the time and won't tell me why!' Alida said outraged

'You... he hasn't been cheating on you! That girl was one of his friends from his old school! He told me last week because I've been helping him and so has she!' I explained, how anyone could, even Alida, be this slow I will never know!

'Oh yeah? What has she been helping him with then?' she asked angrily

'He's been... setting up a surprise for you' I said trying not to give too much away.

'Oh' that's apparently all she could say. After she promised to act surprised when she got it we all walked out and went to find the others. It was true actually. He didn't tell me what the surprise was he just asked me how he could get Alida to a hall somewhere miles away without her suspecting something.

We were all so immersed in our own thoughts that we only remembered about the feathers when Charlie said 'what's the matter with you guys? And why do you look like half a chicken Martin?'

Then we all went our separate ways, Jade and I went back to my house.

I had a shower to get rid of all that sticky rubbish and the feathers then I went downstairs to find Jade lying on the sofa watching another movie. Man does she like her movies! I thought as I sat on her to get her to move.

'Oh, I thought the feathers suited you.' She said when I had sat down and she had leaned on me.

'Thanks! You're really good at this positive reinforcement stuff aren't you?' I replied

'Yep, but I'm good at everything me.'

'Is that so? How interesting... that gives me a few ideas...'

'Ha you wish!'

'You can't blame me for trying! I must say though your aim was very good. What are we watching anyway?' I asked not recognising the few scenes I had seen.

'It's a romance film, basically he-' she pointed to a tall blonde person'- loves her-'she pointed at a rather good looking brunette'- but she's with him-' she pointed to another man but this one was short and ginger'- so he'- she pointed at the blonde guy again'- is going to kill him-' short ginger'- to get with her.' She finished pointing at the women.

'You could put that commentator bloke out of a job if you carry on like that,' I said laughing but she just gave me a light slap. Isn't it amazing I thought how when the TV is off women don't seem to tell you anything and expect you to read their minds but as soon as it's on they never stop talking!

'Oi!' she said and gave me another playful slap

'What did I do?' I asked

'I heard you mumbling something about woman never shutting up when the TV's on' Jade explained.

'Damn!' don't you just hate it when you accidentally say what you're thinking? Especially when it's a sexist comment and you've got your girlfriend sitting next to you?

Then something someone said to me a few years ago just sprang to mind 'there's only one use for a romantic film. To get off with your girl while they are on because you're not going to mind what you miss!' and without noticing I was smiling a lot. Unfortunately Jade did notice.

'How can you be smiling? That guy just had his head ripped off! Are you a sadist or something?' she asked quite scared.

'No it wasn't that I just remembered something'

'What?'

'It doesn't matter'

'No tell me!'

'Don't think so!'

'Just tell me'

'Umm... Na!'

'Tell me!'

'What's in it for me?' I asked for a second time in a week

'Err... huh... I have a few ideas but not just yet...'

'That kinky hey?'

'Who said it was kinky? I didn't, I could have meant a motorbike, ever thought about that?'

'Did you?' I asked

'Well... no but... I could have!'

'But you didn't'

'I know that!' she said poking me

'Are you sure?' I said poking her back.

This might seem a bit strange but we did it all the time, had play fights about completely random things and then have a poking fight afterwards. I'm going to leave the rest of this bit to your imagination and move on.

Chapter 3 - Suggestions of Anal, Friends, Jade and a Little Monster

That Monday I got up as usual except I actually twisted my ankle. I actually took my time getting ready today because I had some of the worst lessons ever, Geography, I.T, History and English... but then again I had P.E last lesson so I guess it's not that bad, and we were playing the girls at rounders.

I got my bike out the shed at about eight o'clock and went out my back gate. I got round the corner from my house and bumped into Jamie one of my best friends from school. It's not surprising that I bump into him a lot because his house is the other side of the road from mine.

'Hey Martin. We really should start looking where we are going.' When I said bumped into him I actually meant I rode into him, I guess I should have been more specific. 'Heard about you having a fight with Jades uncles, is it true you actually hit one of them in the face?'

This shows just how bad peoples hearing is in Bracknell, how does shouting at someone sound like hitting them in the face?

'No I didn't hit either of them in the face, I only shouted at them' I said and I was forced to tell the story again, I was actually starting to find it a bit annoying.

'Wow, your either really, really brave or maybe just stupid... sorry to say it but I'm leaning a bit more towards the stupid.' He said after I had finished.

'Thanks mate! You're a true friend!' I said sarcastically as we got to the bike sheds. 'Anyway I'll see you in P.E'

'See you later' he said. Jamie and I were at two different levels on the social ladder and we hung out with different groups of people. He goes to the library in the mornings and I hang out with my friends Gareth (really annoying at times but a good mate), Keith (yet again good mate but he looks like he's been hit in the face with a shovel, so we call him shovel and it really winds him up), Joe (he's a laugh), Josh (tries to be hard all the time but is really strong) and Charlie (enough said).

Jade didn't hang out with us that much but she occasionally came to the octagons (the octagons is this area with huge concrete octagons in it where you can sit down and hang out, I wonder where they got the name...) to say hi and have a laugh. But mainly she hung out... actually... where does she hang out? Well anyway, she hangs out with Linda, Will and Del... actually speak of the devil...

'Damn! Man that really hurts! Oi Martin!' it was Del and he looked like he had been kicked in the family jewels.

'What did you do?' I asked as he walked towards me.

'I didn't do anything! It's that crazy girlfriend of yours! Can't you keep control of her! She kicked me right in the... well,' he couldn't say the word because my head of year Mr Sanford was just walking past but I kind of got the picture anyway.

'Ok let me rephrase that... what did you do to make her kick you in the privates?' I asked more specifically.

'All I did was subtly suggest I wanted anal se-'

SMACK!

'Hey that was harder than last time!' he shouted outraged.

'Ah but last time you only subtly suggested oral' I said wisely.

'Yeah… well… that was still too hard!' he spluttered finally.

I left him to his moaning and went into the LSU (learning support unit) it's not because were stupid… well I wasn't anyway, it's because there were a few computers in there, comfortable chairs, it was quiet… until we got there anyway but best of all there were hardly any teachers and the ones that were in there liked us so even when all the chavs get kicked out we got to stay.

I got in there said hi to everyone and grabbed a computer before anyone could make me do anything else. The guys were all sat down talking about something but I wasn't listening. I wanted to email Jade to congratulate her for what she did to Del.

'What you doing?' said a voice behind me that made me jump. I turned around only to see Jade standing behind me looking quite pleased with herself.

'E-mailing you actually,' I said kind of annoyed but only a little 'I was going to congratulate you for kicking Del in the balls, but I guess I can do it in person now. What are you up to?' I asked noticing the look on her face.

'Guess what I've got'

'I dunno'

'Guess'

Everyone was watching and listening at this point but I gave them an evil look and they all went about their own business, the power you get from being tall…

Anyway I lead her outside so we wouldn't have everyone eavesdropping on us.

'What is it then?' I asked

'Like I said, guess'

'Umm… is it… something funny?'

'Could be depends what happens there'

'So it's tickets to something?'

'Nope'

'Just tell me!'

'Just guess!' she said in a mocking voice. The person who invented the word guess should be shot.

'Is it something to do with your singing?'

Oh yeah that's what I forgot to tell you, me, Jade, Gareth, Charlie, Keith and some other people were in a band together but also Jade does solo singing with her performance group called 'Stage'. Every now and again they would put on a play or sing somewhere.

'Yes'

'You've got a solo in the next play?'

'A bit bigger than that... I've got a recording contract!' she shouted with so much happiness that she must have cheered up the whole world.

'You're kidding? You're not kidding? Wow, well done! You finally got your big break!' I said and gave her a kiss and a huge hug. I was so happy for her it felt like I was the one with the contract.

'Can you come with me to the recording studio after school?' she asked

'I'm sure I can manage that. I mean my sister will kill me but I'm sure she'll understand, it's not every day your girlfriend gets a recording contract is it?'

'Good' she said then she went to the library to tell the others

'Gareth, just to let you know I can't come round yours after school today sorry.' I said when I got back into the LSU.

'That's the third time in a row that you've cancelled and I bet it's for Jade!' he said quite angrily, I don't know why he was so angry, I mean all we ever do is play on the PS2. 'So what's your excuse this time? Jade broke a nail and you need to take her to hospital?'

'No actually she got a recording contract and I'm going with her to the recording studio!' I said just as angrily.

'Yeah right!'

'You either believe me, or you don't! Either way it doesn't affect my decision! Jade has a recording contract and I'm going with her to the studio after school!' I argued

'You're... you're serious about her aren't you?' he asked in shock

'Finally noticed have you? That's slow even for you!' I shouted still fuming.

'You swear she actually has this... contract?'

'I swear'

'Then let me come with you just to prove it. I'll stay out of the way.' he said.

'It's not me you have to ask its Jade. If she hasn't got a problem with it then neither do I'

'I'll go ask her then' he said and he left to go find her.

I turned around to start talking to Charlie when I heard Gareth's voice again 'By the way... where is she?'

'Library' I answered without looking at him, I still felt quite angry with him.

'You know what? You're right, you do have an anger problem,' Charlie said to me. I'd had an anger problem since I was little but nobody ever thought that I did because I was so nice and was always in control of it. I was good at keeping it inside, it's like a monster, always trying to get out but I was very strong willed and I had only ever let it half out and even then it's not nice. Last time I lost it I hit a boy in the face, threw another against a tree and kicked another in the stomach as he was jumping at me. I really hated that side of me and so far I have managed not to let Jade see that side, I think we wouldn't be as happy if she ever saw that side. I thought to myself.

'I'm sorry but when Gareth blames things on Jade when it's my fault it really gets to me, it gets to me if anyone does anything that would upset her that's why I've never lost it in front of her because that will upset her' I said thoughtfully, 'Promise me if I ever look like I'm about to lose it in front of Jade you will calm me down.'

'Sure,' he said simply, 'I never believed you had an anger problem because you are always so… nice.' (Told you, coincidence… I think so)

'That wasn't me as angry as I can be that was only the monster sniffing the air.'

'What monster? Who said anything about a monster? You know I don't like monsters!' he said in a joking voice.

That made me smile at least, Charlie was always funny especially when you needed him to be… and especially when you didn't…

'Anyway what's this about a recording contract?' Keith asked.

'Oh, Jade has got a recording contract' I said

'Yeah I kind of gathered that, when? Where? How?' he said

'To tell you the truth I don't know, all I know is she's got one and we are going to the studio after school.' I replied.

'Cool, are you sure it's not a joke?' Keith asked

'No because I can read Jade like a book, she was really excited and nervous. Remember that song about how you can tell if people are lying by their kiss? Yeah well hers isn't any different so I'm guessing she's telling the truth. Oh yeah and the fact that I would trust her with my life.' I finished.

'Well… good luck to her. Maybe she can help get us a contract as well, what do you think?' Charlie said

'I don't think so,' Keith said 'but you are going to have to look out for her when you're there Martin, these music people only want to rip people off. That's what all business men are like so you might have to stand up to them like you stood up to her uncles.' He finished

'Good point… well… coming from a shovel anyway…' I said and he threw a cushion at me.

Jade was hyper all day but for some reason she didn't tell many people, but you know what schools like so by the end of the day everyone in our class knew and as we headed out the school gates everyone was shouting good luck.

We went to my house, so I could get changed and as usual nobody was home. We got up and walked out the back door and then I just followed her from there In case we were riding there.

'So where is the studio anyway?' I asked as we went towards her house presumably to get a lift from her mum.

'In London, we have to go to my house and wait for my mum to get home from work. We'll probably leave a couple of hours after that.' She said in response

'Why do we have to wait a couple of hours?' I asked

'We have to wait for Gareth and he always used to get lost,' she said. Oh yea that's another thing I forgot to mention, Jade and Gareth went out in year 7. Gareth accused her of cheating on him with Will, which was nonsense, and they hated each other until I started the band in year 8 and needed a singer and there she was right in front of me. 'He has a really bad sense of direction and too much pride to ask for directions.'

'So he is coming then? Did he tell you about our little fight?'

'Yes he is and no he didn't. He didn't need to I heard you two from the library, sounded quite big. Was that you angry?' she had a fascination with trying to see me fully angry which didn't help considering I didn't want her to and never planned on letting her.

'No it wasn't that was hardly anything, I didn't even have to hit anything afterwards. Although I guess he would have been the first candidate.' 'Why do you want to see me angry anyway? You got scared when I was annoyed remember?'

It was true, I didn't manage to keep totally calm that time but I didn't let too much out.

'Yeah... that was scary... but I want to know because I'm supposed to know everything about you, every side of you, how you feel and all that stuff.' This was also true but I was ashamed of the other side of me, why couldn't she understand that?

We got to her house and put our bikes in the garage, and then I thought I should really call home before they call the police, that's happened too many times before. So I got out my mobile and noticed that I had a message

Hey Martin its Alex

Just wunderin weva u wanted do some archery in the woods on Sunday, Edds coming n so iz Nathan

t.b (b4 Sunday preferably)

C ya

My friend Alex and I normally went to the woods every other week so we can practice Javelin or archery. It was quite fun but very hazardous because we normally made our own bows and arrows and we made loads of arrows and had a fight afterwards. He normally won because I'm such a big target but if Edd and Nathan were going that means that we would team up against them and kick there asses.

I text back saying sure what time and then called home to tell them what was happening with Jade.

Gareth unusually turned up early. He must be ready for another fight... or he just got a lift from his mum. He was very quiet at Jades but that could just be because nobody in the house except me and Jade liked him, but I was starting to be one of those who didn't.

'Look, I'm sorry for what I said at school, it was out of order and I really don't want to lose you as a mate. So forgive and forget?' he said after fifteen minutes.

Wow! An apology from Gareth... that's never happened before... but that could be because we have never argued before... he has been a good mate all these years... I guess I should forgive him...

'Forgive and forget. I hate arguing with people especially my best mates but you can understand why I cancelled don't you?'

'Yeah of course I do, I just... well I guess I got a bit jealous that you guys were spending so much time together but that's natural now you're going out.' He said

'Tell you what... what about Saturday?' I asked him

'What about it?' he said, he really was quite dim

'Do you want to come round on Saturday? I'm sure me and Jade can be separated for a day or two' I said sarcastically

'Guys...' I heard Jade mumble

'Oi! Gaz help me tickle her, you remember where she's really ticklish right?'

'Of course' and with that we both tickled her only to get kicked off the sofa and get bundled by Jade and Hayley.

There was a knock at the door and Jades mum answered it. All I heard is some really camp sounding guy say 'mother darling,' and then there was the sound of two kisses on the cheek and then the same voice say 'Where is she?'

By this time Gaz and me had moved to the doorway and peeked around the corner. There was a man with very bright multi-coloured trousers on, a fur coat, sunglasses and a bright pink shirt with a tie of the most vibrant purple I had ever seen. Gaz and I looked at each other, went in the sitting room, closed the door and fell about on the floor laughing our heads off.

'What are you laughing at?' Hayley asked. She went to have a look and then fell on the floor laughing as well.

The door opened and we quickly composed ourselves and made it look like we were looking for something.

'What are you three doing?' Jades mum asked

'We... are ... err... trying to find... the remote for the TV.' I said, I think I strained my brain then... over use.

'It's on top of the TV.' She said pointing

'Well... that would explain why we couldn't find it on the floor.' Gaz said also thinking hard.

'Right well anyway this is Marcus Davigi. He is the one who offered Jade the contract. Mr Davigi, this is Hayley, Jades sister. Gareth, one of Jades school friends. And this is Martin, Jades boyfriend.' She finished the introductions.

'So this is the one who will be in the publicity shots with Jade' he said, publicity shots? I hate having my photo taken! I'll just have to persevere...

'Yes that's him' Jades mum said.

'When are we going to the studio?' Jade asked Mr Davigi

'Oh did your mother not tell you? We are going to stay here to brief you about what is going to happen over the next few months.' He replied, for some reason he hesitated before saying this... Do I know this guy? I'm sure I recognise him... I thought

'Oh... ok never mind then. So what is going to happen?' Jade asked.

'Well first you need a manager-'he started

'I've got one. Martin is the manager for our band and he's done right by me and the others and has never done anything without running it past us first.' She finished and I felt my face get a bit hotter.

'Is that so? Well I doubt he has all the contacts our managers have, for example,' he said turning to me 'do you have any contacts on TV shows or newspapers? The numbers of any famous people prepared to sponsor her? Are you on good terms with any other bands or singers that are on tour?' I shook my head; I had tried my best to get gigs for the band and had got a couple but no famous contacts. 'I didn't think you would. To even think you could manage any band or person without good contacts... I pity you, I really do.'

Who does he think he is? Of course I don't have any famous contacts, I'm in school! He can keep his pity for someone who needs it! I thought my anger levels rising a little wait Martin, calm down, this is Jade's big shot and we don't want to mess it up. I told myself. Stupid conscience.

'Well... if not him then who?' Jade asked

'We have dozens of managers at your disposal and all of them have many, many contacts that could help.' He finished, is he trying to annoy me? I really don't like this guy! 'However since you are so young all the managers will insist on twenty percent instead of the usual ten because it will take a lot more work to get people to take you seriously.'

'Sorry but I'm not having this!' the monster was sniffing again.

'Martin just leave it, it's fine honestly.' Jade said to me

'Are you sure?' I said dragging her into the corner so we could have a private conversation. 'This guy... Dashivi-'

'Davigi' Jade corrected me

'Close enough, anyway he thinks he can take advantage of you because you are younger than his normal clients, don't let him walk all over you'

'Martin, do you really think I'm doing this for the money? He can have fifty percent if he wants I don't really care about the money.' She said

'You really are too nice for your own good' I whispered

'I know' she replied and we went back to the others

'Any problems?' Jades mum asked

'No. Where were we?' Jade said before I could say anything

'Ok so the manager has been sorted out' said Davigi looking at me 'now, what sort of music do you normally sing?'

'In the band we do Indy or rock' she said

'Nope! We can't have that, you now sing pop music.' Davigi said. I looked at Jade giving her one of those looks that says can I hit him yet? But she shook her head so I kept my mouth shut, for her sake.

'I can live with that' she said, First I'm not a good manager! Then he rips her off! Now he's changing her style of music! I don't like this one bit! I thought I am so tempted just so kick him and his multi-coloured trousers out the window of a forty eight-story building!

'Ok now your fashion... hmm... well there a lot of improvement needed.' That's out of order her fashion is brilliant! She's the most fashionable person I know! Anyway what does he know about fashion? By the looks of things not much! 'Don't get me wrong your fashion has a lot of... potential but it's not what we are looking for, so you might want to have a look at the fabric sample I've got here'

And then he pulled some scraps of fabric out of somewhere in his coat. One was bright pink, Jade hates pink surely she's going to say something now, the other was a very murky brown, well that one's screwed, and the last was Burberry! Now she's gunna say something for sure!

'All fine' she said

'You what?! Jade can I have a word? Hayley and Gaz can you come too?' I asked and dragged them into the back garden 'I'm sorry but this has gone too far!'

'He's right Jade you shouldn't have to change who you are.' Hayley agreed

'And all that stuff about you doing pop, can't see it myself,' Gaz said 'anyway why aren't you standing up for yourself? And why are you stopping Martin from kicking his ass?'

'Because this is my big break! I can live with all that stuff' she mumbled quietly

'But the point we are trying to make is you shouldn't have to! You are a great person; your voice is phenomenal when you're singing your style you have great fashion sense and he's trying to turn you into a chav!' I said

'Please guys just let me do this my way?' she pleaded. We looked at each other.

'Ok... but if he does one more thing to annoy me, don't expect me to stay quiet about it. You know you wanted to see me angry? Well put it this way, I only need one more nudge!' I said. This was true enough, his belly only held the monster in.

'Fine, but try not to trash the house if you lose it' she said in a very worried voice.

'Yeah that's a good point! I've seen the cracks in your wall where you keep hitting it! Try to vent your anger on him not the house' Gaz said and we all laughed, apart from me, I was going back inside thinking. Part of me wanted him to push me over the edge but then another part of me wanted to keep Jade from seeing me like that and then there was a little one at the back of my head saying I swear I've seen him before, where do I know him from?

We got back in there and I heard him say to Jades mum '...over protective boyfriends aren't good for publicity or singing careers...'

I instantly turned around and went back outside. I went round the corner and punched the wall a couple of times to vent the anger I went to hit it again but Jade came around the corner and I stopped myself. I suddenly became very conscious of the fact that tears of rage were falling down my cheeks, but it was also helped by the fact that my hand was killing.

She walked up to me and I just looked at the ground not wanting her to see me like this. She hugged me and then grabbed my hands that I couldn't get out of fists. I looked at her through my blurry eyes; she was calm as she could be even if there was fear in her eyes.

'I'm sorry Martin but this is how it has to be if I have a chance at making it. Please just give him one more chance? For me?'

I couldn't speak I just looked at the floor and nodded. She gave me a minute or two to compose myself and pull the little stones out of my fist then she lead the way back into the lounge.

'Well are we all ok?' the man who had all my hatred at the moment said, I ignored him and sat on the sofa next to Jade with Gaz on the other side of me. He looked at my fists and started to say something but I just shook my head to signal for him not to say anything.

'No but I'm sure we can manage' Jade said looking at me with a worried expression on her face.

'Ok...' he said for some reason looking quite pleased with himself, 'well anyway there is one more thing we need to sort out, we need to give you an attitude... maybe a naughty girl kind of thing or maybe... a bit of a... sleep with anything kind of look... yeah that could wor-'

SMASH!

I couldn't help it he just pushed me way to far this time. 'Ok, you can do or say anything you want to do with me but I am not going to let you change Jade into a... a chavy slut!' I roared, now it had started nothing was going to stop it 'I am not going to stand for you ripping her off! You are trying to do the impossible! You're trying to improve upon perfection! Well guess what... it isn't gunna happen! She may be able to stand it but I can't! We need to get a few things straight-'Smack! '- That's for trying to change Jades style-'Smack! '- That's for trying to change her-'Smack! '- That's for trying to make her out to be a slut! And this-'Smack! '- Is for making me show Jade the side of me I hate the most!' I finished and walked out the house.

'Stop!' I heard Davigi shout at me but I didn't look back I just carried on. 'I said stop!'

I still carried on until I heard a much softer voice shout my name.

'Martin, Martin wait' I stopped and leant my back on a wall and slid down until I was sitting.

'Do you see now? Do you see why I didn't want you to see that side of me?' I said when she stopped in front of me.

'I-I never knew you had that much anger inside of you' she said in a voice so quiet it was barely more than a whisper.

'I didn't, at least not until he started talking' I said unable to stop the tears streaming out of my eyes.

'I'm sorry I asked you to come here Martin this is all my fault,' she said and sat down next to me.

'It's not your fault, honestly. If I could go back in time and do this again there is only one thing I would change, I would make sure you're not in the room when I did that.'

'Sounds like something you would say,' she said still barely more than a whisper.

'I'm sorry, I ruined your chances of making it haven't I?' I asked

'Not really, I guess you were right, I didn't want things to be the way he described it. Anyway I've still got you and the band to help make it. I'd prefer to be in a band anyway, there's less pressure on you.' She really is amazing, always knows how to make people feel better.

We walked back to her house having made me calm down and stop crying. We walked in through the front door and there was Davigi but... he wasn't Davigi... it was Damien one of Jades uncles! That's why I recognised him; he was just wearing a wig, glasses and all the weird clothes. Oh Damn! That's just my luck! Now I'm never going to get his approval!

'Hello again' he said quite calmly holding the side of his head where I had punched him a lot, 'you know what? You've got one hell of a punch boy'

I just froze, I was completely stunned. I looked at Jade and her face was full of anger so not surprisingly she slapped him and went off to her room crying.

I went up to see Jade about five minutes later after I had had it explained to me. I found her on her bed crying her eyes out. I sat on the bed next to her and she sat up and looked at me.

'Come here' I said and gave her a hug, saying supportive things like its ok and all that stuff.

'I can't believe him!' she sobbed 'my own flesh and blood using my dream against me!'

'I know, I know,' it turned out that Damien and Kevin had set this whole thing up to see whether they would approve of me. They wanted to see if I'd do the best thing for Jade whether she realised it or not. They didn't tell Jade because they were told, presumably by Jade's mum, that I can read her like a book… and the fact that she's a really bad liar, but we won't mention that because this is supposed to be one of those really soppy endings.

Anyway I explained it all to Jade from her uncles' point of view, agreed that they were prats and that they… well the most polite way of putting it is that they weren't very nice. But as it is with most girls, she forgave him after a couple of weeks. (Have you noticed that? Women have arguments all the time but end up friends with again by the end of the month. And you would end up looking really stupid afterwards because you don't pay any attention anymore, she would say something about how someone's really nice and you would say 'But I thought you weren't talking to her?' and then she would say 'No! We made up weeks ago! You really don't listen to me do you?' and then you would try to explain it and just end up looking like a prat anyway. Women!)

Have you noticed I always seem to get angry when Jades uncles are involved? I know I'm criticising my own story but somebody's got to do it. Well anyway on to the next part of the story.

Chapter 4 - Blood and Bows

On Saturday I went round Gaz's house like I said I would and we had a laugh annoying his little sister and having contests on the PS2. It was fun and I'm glad I went because I needed cheering up after what happened at Jades house.

On Sunday I woke up at about half past eleven (I'm a teenager, it's expected of me, I can't let the side down now can I?). I got up got dressed and went downstairs to watch TV; I was flicking through the channels, as you do when nothing is on, until I saw an advert with Robin Hood in it, Crap I was supposed to be doing archery today! Where's my phone? Did I have it yesterday? No I got moaned at because I left it here. Where is it? Man Alex is gunna kill me if I'm late! Is that it? No that's the remote for the TV! Where is it?

Bleep bleep!

Yes the battery is dying! Now where did those bleeps come from?

Bleep bleep!

Behind me? Oh yea I remember it's in my room! I was using it to take photos of photos; well I need to have copies these days because Jade ripped up a few of the ones of her that I had. Not that she's insecure or anything...

I found it and saw there was a message but then the battery gave up and died. You- now calm down, it's a phone and the battery died. All you need to do is find the charger... where's the charger? I hate this house! You can never find anything! Wait hold on... the charger should be by the computer... but then again nothings where it should be so I'll check my room first.

So I tore my room apart trying to find the charger. When I had finished it was quarter past twelve. And guess what else! The charger was where it was supposed to be! That's what I get for trying to be smart!

Anyway once it had enough battery to let me check my messages it turned out that there were two new ones, one from Alex and the other from Charlie. I checked the one from Charlie first.

Hey you lazy slacker!

Y ent u awake yet? U r never up on a weekend!

Neway wanted 2 no if u wanted to come round mine on Tuesday after school so we can hang out and catch up on girl stuff coz we don't talk bout that stuff at skl

Tb sayin weva u want 2 or not.

C ya at skl

Well I had to go to that because we used to talk about girls at school, mainly about which girls were fit and who had the nicest butt or the biggest breasts but then me, Charlie and Gaz got girlfriends and we had to stop for obvious reasons. But I couldn't make it this Tuesday as I had family stuff to sort out so I text him back rescheduling for next Tuesday.

Anyway the text from Alex was short and simple and god damn annoying! All it said was a time, a time that was about twenty minutes ago!

I got my trainers on, grabbed my bow and arrows from the back shed and ran as fast as my legs would carry me, which wasn't very fast but still, I should at least get points for trying.

I got there at quarter-to-one and they had obviously started without me because all I saw on the way to the woods was an arrow fly up above the trees and fall back down. Then there was an almighty cry of pain and I ran even faster into the forest.

'Nathan you son of a-'

'Really ugly mother!' I interrupted Edd my cousin

'Martin glad you finally made it' Alex said to me while Edd sniggered and Nathan looked puzzled trying to work out what I said. Alex was probably my best friend, I could trust him with anything and he helped me whenever I needed it and was always a laugh especially when you needed him to be. 'What took so long?'

'Long story short my battery went dead and I couldn't find the charger.'

'Sounds like your house! Nothings ever where it's supposed to be!' Edd said. Edd was my cousin but he was as good as a brother to me. There were something's about him that annoyed me though like the fact that he is half a year younger than me but has always been half a head taller! Not that I need to be any taller but he could do with shrinking a bit, let's be honest, six foot five is a bit much for a fourteen year old.

'You know what? That's exactly what I said, well that's what I thought anyway but you know what I mean.' I said

'Talking about what you said, what did you say about my f****** mum you b******?' Nathan asked looking a bit bewildered

'Don't worry Nathan you just go back to sleep' I said mockingly.

'I would do but this mother f***** woke me up this morning' he replied pointing at Alex. There one thing you need to know about Nathan, he can't say a single sentence without swearing so I'll just put stars where the swear words are so I don't offend Queeny.

'Anyway who shot that arrow; I could see it on my way up here!' I asked

'That was Nathan!' Edd replied hotly 'He bet he could get it higher than the trees and we put a fiver on it. So he got it higher than the trees and I'm now skint.'

'So who shouted?'

'That was Edd' Alex explained 'the arrow Nathan shot came back down and got Edd's foot!' he finished trying not to crack up laughing.

Well they are big targets, he had size fourteen feet! It's not any wonder that the kids picked on him when I arrived in Bracknell. But then he started hanging out with me and I'm quite intimidating when I want to be so they left him alone. But then as soon as I went to Brakenhale he had to try and fend for himself in Easthampsted Park (EP for short), and he didn't do great at that. For the most part (from what I could gather anyway) he hung out with younger kids because they thought he was cool... oh how misled they were.

'Well shall we get started? Blunt arrows only guys!' I always had to make sure they put down the sharp ones. We used the sharp ones for target practice when we shot tin cans or other targets (I bet when I said about archery you thought we did it like professionals, shows what you know). Ok so I know it's like a health and safety horror show, firing homemade arrows from homemade bows at each other but we're blokes, what do you expect?

So I ran behind a tree and tried to climb it while Alex covered me. I got up to a good vantage point and covered Alex while he climbed up. Now, this is a good plan because you get the height so they can't hide as well but there is one problem with this tactic... you run out of arrows and have to jump down to collect them again and that's when Edd and Nathan shoot us... well actually... Edd was shooting at us while Nathan kept firing before he could aim. Turned out Edd was in more danger of Nathan than we were.

Alex and I were running low on arrows again so we dropped out of the tree and grabbed all the arrows we could while running behind some other trees. Alex and me reloaded our bows and jumped out at the same time and shot. I got Nathan in the arm while Alex... well if you're a guy prepare to cringe... got Edd in the Crown Jewels. He fell to the floor and I just applauded Alex's marvellous shot.

Edd got up rather red in the face, he saw the sharpened arrows on the floor and grabbed one and knocked it. He took aim at Alex and fired. Now this is the bit where we all point and laugh at Edd. He aimed for Alex yes but the arrow went for me! If I hadn't been for my quick reactions then I would have been blinded but it just cut the side if my face. I ended up with quite a deep cut all across the left of my face.

'Great shot orang-utan!' I yelled in rage. The reason for calling him this isn't because he's big orange and hairy (that's only part of it) his mother Beverley... well... she has a... strange sense of humour. His whole name is actually Edward Joshuah-Tree-orgustus-Cornelius-orang-utan-pertang-pertang-oley-oley-biscuit-barrel Hawthorne. We still don't know her original hair colour (or planet) but I expected it was blonde (well as the saying goes, men are from mars, women are from Venus and Beverley is from Alpha Centauri).

'How the hell? I was aiming for Alex! How does that work?' he shouted outraged that he missed.

'It works because your aim isn't much better than Nathan's!' Alex said laughing.

'Ah, but you admit I am better, well... that's not hard is it, you have to train day and night to miss the broad side of a barn by as much as Nathan does' laughed Edd, as Nathan threw a stone at Edd, and, guess what? HE HIT! Miracles do happen! Well, he hit something, but what made it even better is that he hit himself, 'God Bless the man who put that tree there!'

They are all very considerate, they stand there talking about how Nathan can't shoot at the floor and hit, meanwhile I was there on the floor in agony, blood pouring down my face and neck.

We all went home laughing (well they did anyway) and reminiscing about how Edd and Nathan get their butts kicked every time. We all went our separate ways at Edd's house, which conveniently is just down the road from my house, literally. Edd went in and I went to the hospital, stupid stitches. I know girls are supposed to love scars and everything but I bet Jade is gunna freak!

Chapter 5 - The Past Catches Up With You Eventually

I went round Charlie's house the next Tuesday after Edd's... unfortunate accident.

I walked up to his house, which strangely enough was the same number as mine even though he lived in Wild Ridings and I lived in Great Hollands, and knocked on the door.

His brother Carl answered the door. 'Urgh! What do you want?' he asked as soon as he saw that it was me. Carl was cool, the sort of person you don't want to get on the wrong side of, but when he wasn't being macho hard man he was quite funny.

'Good to see you to Carl, is your brother in?'

'Yea I'll just get him.' And he turned away and a couple of minutes later another Bateman was at the door.

'Oh hey Martin, I take it you want Charlie?' it was Dan Charlie's other brother holding his daughter Caitlin, 'Carls annoying sometimes'

'What do you mean sometimes?'

'Good point. Caitlin, do you want to call Charlie?' he asked his daughter. She wasn't even two yet but she could talk pretty well for someone of her age.

'Yea! Charwie!' she shouted back into the house.

Then all you heard was Charlie shout back 'Caitlin' and him walking down the stairs.

'Smelly!' she said pointing at me, Carl had taught her to call me smelly a couple of months ago.

'Oh hey Martin' he said poking his head round the door 'come in, we'll have to go upstairs the house is kind of full'

We went up to his room to find Gaz already there.

'Hey Gaz, you alright?' I said sitting on the office chair that I always span on when I got bored.

'Hey I'm goo- what happened to your face?' he asked he hadn't been at school all week so I had to explain the story again; I had already had to tell the story at least a dozen times at school. Some people felt sorry for me, some laughed, some (Jade in the lead) wanted to hurt Edd (when you're a nice guy you make a lot of really good friends)

'I'm alright; I thought you would be with Christy though. You're normally inseparable at school.' Christine was in the story earlier but I only mentioned her name so I'll tell you what she's like now. She is one of those can be funny people that put on a strong, 'don't mess with me' appearance but she is a very nice person it you can get past the tough exterior.

'Na, she's gone to the sea side with her family, stupid family' he mumbled

'Oh well let's talk then, you know like we used t-' Charlie started to say but I put my hand up to indicate for him to shut up a minute. I had done this because I could hear a buzzing. I had a look under Charlie's bed and, like I thought, there was a tape recorder taped under it recording our conversation. I stopped it and pulled it out to show the other two.

'Now two possibilities. One; Carl put this in here so he could black mail us.' I said after turning the tape recorder off 'Two; the girls somehow got in here and put it here or got Alex to put it here.'

By the way Alex was Carl's girlfriend.

'But the girls don't know we were planning on doing this... did they?' Gaz looked at Charlie and then me.

'I didn't tell... what's her name again...? I keep forgetting... Sally?' Charlie said more to himself than us.

'Your girlfriend's name is Sarah. You're worse than me!' I said 'but back to the point, there's always the chance that Sarah or Jade read the texts on our phones'

'True... but I'm still betting its Carl's handy work.' Gaz said thoughtfully.

'It wasn't me' said Carls voice from the landing 'Damn!'

'Get him!' Charlie shouted and we ran after him and chased him to the park where I rugby tackled him and the other two jumped on him.

In the end... well the easy way to say it is that... we lost. In our defence however he was really strong. We all went back to Charlie's house with our battle scars. I was limping and had a dead arm, Charlie was going to have a black eye the next day and was cut in several places and Gaz was walking like an old man because Carl had killed his back.

When we got back we just went up to Charlie's room and played games for about an hour until there was a knock at the front door.

Charlie ran to get it but Carl beat him there. 'What do you want?' I heard Carl say from Charlie's room.

'Is Charlie there?' asked a very polite girls voice, a voice that I'm sure I knew from somewhere but couldn't remember where. I had heard it quite a few years ago... but where?

'Hi Sarah' I heard Charlie say and then there was a big bang which indicated that Charlie had just shoulder barged his brother into the wall.

'That was uncalled for!' I heard Carl say. By this time Gaz and I were listening at Charlie's bedroom door.

'Come upstairs there's some people I want you to meet.' Charlie said and led the way upstairs. Me and Gaz hurriedly sat on the bed at this point and pretended to be playing the game. He opened the door and said 'Guys this is-'

'Sarah!' I interrupted.

'Martin? What are you doing here?' Sarah asked

'I take it you two know each other already?' Charlie said a bit bewildered

'Yeah me and Sarah where best mates when I lived in Farnborough but what are you doing here? I haven't heard from you in years.'

'Now I'm sure I asked you that question first.' She replied

'Yeah but you know, ladies first.' She always tried to teach me to be a gentleman in primary school and always said things like ladies first.

'Ah but men just before if I remember correctly' she said, that's what I always said back to her if I couldn't be bothered to let ladies go first. Women.

'Fine, be that way! I'm round one of my best friend's house having a laugh with a couple of friends. Now it's your turn.'

'I'm round my boyfriend's house because I just got back from holiday' she replied. 'What happened to you guys anyway?'

'long story' Charlie said obviously not wanting to remember the pain of that memory ever again 'So how do you two know each other?' he asked when we had all sat down.

'Well Sarah was going out with one of my friends at school,' I explained 'and we found we had loads in common and started hanging out a bit more. Then a couple of weeks after we started hanging out her boyfriend, Antony Gay, started getting jealous and we kind of... haven't talked to each other since'

'Well actually once you moved to Somerset me and Antony became friends again and went out again until he got jealous of another of my friends only this time it was a girl.' Sarah said

'Did he? Now I knew he wasn't exactly bright but... that's bad even for him! He's even dumber than Gaz and that's saying something.' He never tried getting in contact with me after I moved but that's because he thought I was with Sarah as well as him and he held grudges for a long time. It had never even crossed my mind to ask Sarah out because I never felt about her that way, which was strange because when I've not got a girlfriend I'm a natural flirt... or so I've been told.

'I didn't know that you moved to Bracknell though, last I heard you were still in Somerset.' Sarah said looking at me.

'No I moved here a few years ago. I take it you did as well?'

'Yeah about three months ago...' so the rest of the day was spent with me and Sarah reminiscing in the corner while Charlie and Gaz played the game. Charlie didn't seem to mind too much though, admittedly Sarah had been known to spend eight hours on the phone but I was a good listener which is another reason we got on so well.

Oh well that's another character to add to an already complicated story, why do I do it to myself?

Chapter 6 - Starlight (Sounds So Magical)

A few weeks later I got a call from the people at the local under-sixteen club.

'Hello, is this Martin Hill?'

'Yeah who's this?' I asked, half paying attention whilst watching a car program on the TV. I'd spent the day looking after my little cousin George, he seemed to look up to me so he spent the day tailing me and I tried to include him while Edd and my other cousin DJ tried anything they could to get rid of him, eventually leading to them getting rid of me. Being nice is hard but George is a funny kid so it's not all bad.

'It's Freddy McNeal, the owner of the Starlight under-sixteen night club in Aldershot.'

'Really... never heard of it, how did you get my number?' I still had the memory of being lied to by Jade's uncle so I was being suspicious.

'I was talking to a friend of mine who saw your band play at your school in October. He was very impressed so he did some digging around, talked to the owner of the pub in which you played for someone's birthday party and got your number. He then gave it to me with a very high recommendation.' He finished, I was impressed, he obviously knew what he was doing.

'Well you found me. How may I help you?' I said suddenly very business-like.

'Well we are offering you a slot at the club, we pay very well and it will be good publicity for you and the others. Would you like to take the slot? It will last forty-five minutes and then we will have another band on.'

'Well I'll have to consult the band, I'm sure you understand. We have practice on Friday I'll ask them then and get back to you. May I ask when the slot is?'

'It will be on the twenty first of July, from seven until nine. Will that be ok?' he asked me.

'If we can make it, then yes that will be fine. I will need some way of contacting you...' so then we swapped contact details and I went back to what I was doing. That wasn't the first time someone had called me to arrange a gig and wouldn't be the last so it wasn't anything unusual. We hadn't played at a club before though; we mainly played at parties, social events and at school.

I went into the practice rooms on Friday, which is these rooms we have at school that are sound proofed so we wouldn't distract anyone else during our practical work in music. Miss Phelps always let us use them for practice because the other teachers didn't really want Gaz's drumming distracting them from their marking.

'Hey guys got a proposition for you. I got called by this guy, Freddy something, who wanted us to play for him. Are you up for it?'

'Where is it? Not another pub! Last time we barely made it out alive!' Keith said. It was perfectly true, we went in there and halfway through our fourth song a couple of people started a fight and the whole pub joined in. we grabbed our equipment and ran to the van as fast as we could. Lucky a few of our parents had stayed and helped us with the instruments and gave us a lift home. It wasn't all bad though, we got paid double for the inconvenience.

'No it's an under-sixteen club in Aldershot, moon fight or somethi-'

'Not Starlight! Was that the name?' Alexandra, Alex for short, asked sounding excited. Alex was short tempered, strong and a bass player... not a good mix.

'Yeah that's the one why?'

'Have you never heard of Starlight? It's the best club for teenagers in Berkshire and a couple other counties!' Louise said. Louise was mental to say the least, she came to band because everyone else did... well at first anyway then she appointed herself our hair dresser. She wasn't too bad either and she was a laugh.

'I've been there before, really easy to get laid' said a voice from the corner.

'Del! What the hell are you doing here?' I asked

'What the hell are you doing here?' he replied

'We have band practice here every week! You should know you're on the security team at the gigs! You didn't answer my question'

'I dunno, I was planning on scaring your girlfriend but she just invited me in here.'

'That is not what happened!' Charlie butted in 'I saw it he tried to suggest some form of sex and Jade kicked him in the balls and he hasn't moved since.'

'Not "hasn't moved"... more like not able to...' he said looking at the floor.

'Well that would explain why he's huddled on the floor...' I didn't quite know what to say 'good work Jade'

'Thank you, I thought my evil look would be enough but this was much more fun.' She said with a sadistic smile, she really worried me sometimes... 'So anyway about this gig, I would be up for it if everyone else is' there was a murmur of yes and sure 'well that settles it. When is it and how long for?' you got to love the way she takes control of the situation when it's deteriorating.

'It's on the twenty first of July from seven till nine' I said trying to remember 'that doesn't give us long to sort out a play list and lifts.'

'Can't we borrow your brothers van to get the stuff there?' Gaz asked me. My brother Aaron did have a van and normally helped us shift our stuff when we had a gig, he works for my uncles delivery company and is a right laugh even if you're fighting him.

'Probably, can everyone else get a lift? If not we might have to see about jumping in with someone else' this is what normally happened when we couldn't get to a gig on foot. Gaz and Charlie wouldn't be able to get a lift and sometimes Louise, so they would arrange to go with someone else. Then that person would remember when they were halfway there, that they had to pick them up and had to turn around get them. Well what do you expect? What do you take us for? Organised?

When we all went to set up our instruments for practice, as I thought, Charlie and Gaz came up to me and said 'Martin, now you know I've been your good friend for many years? Any chance of a lift to the gig?'

'How did I know it would be you two who asked?' it was just like them, 'I'm sure I can arrange something. Why do you two always come to me for a lift anyway?'

'Because when we arrange to get a ride from Jade she normally forgets' said Charlie.

'And when she finally remembers she blames us for her forgetting!' Gaz butted in.

'Alex is normally taking Louise and Jasmine' Charlie said. Jasmine is basically another Louise; we couldn't find a job for her so she appointed herself our fashion designer. I know, I know it's quite sad but I felt guilty her not having something to do. She was really nice though, always ready to help and would be first to help you in a fight if Alex wasn't the person who started it. She was in army cadets because she wanted to be in the army, well, obviously but I've got to say these things to make it clear. Anyway Alex, Louise and Jasmine were all in year ten the year above us even though, and this was a proven fact, me, Andy and Jade were smarter than them.

Anyway Gaz spoke next, 'and my dad's always working and so is my mum.'

'And my mum and dad just can't be bothered' Charlie finished before I could say anything.

'Why don't you go with Keith?' I asked

'Well the problem with that… his parents don't like us as much as they like you, everyone's parents like you. Still don't see why. I mean me and Gaz are way funnier.'

This was true enough, they were always the comedians and all my jokes were… well let's say that Jade says they suck big fat donkey toes, enough said really.

'I guess, but on one condition.' I said giving in but not without a fight.

'Uh oh, this is where he charges us more than a couple of taxis would. You never think of anyone else do you?' said Charlie.

'Ok two things, one that's rich coming from you, you never helped someone unless you get paid for it and two I wasn't going to charge you I was just going to say that you make sure Sarah and Christy can make their own way there because there will be no room in the car because my mum is looking after John that night.' John was my nephew; he was one and a half at that time and was really, really funny. If you said he was being cheeky he would walk up to you, grab your cheek and say cheeky back to you. He was brilliant… until he throws up… in your mouth… bad day… don't ask…

'Can we manage that?' Charlie asked Gaz

'Maybe, if we push ourselves a little'

'Why would you push yourself? You'd get a face full of dirt!'

'Actually how could you push yourself? You'd like, have to detach your arms… that would hurt'

'Actually it wouldn't hurt; your arm would go numb. You need both ends of the nerve to feel the pain, my dad told me.' Charlie said thoughtfully, for the first time in his life he said something smart that could possibly be true.

'Yeah but your dad has about as much brains as a peanut'

'Is that right?' Charlie said trying to raise himself to Gaz's height which was difficult for him.

'Yeah it is!' Gaz replied making himself even taller 'why got a problem with that?'

'Maybe I have!' Charlie said and he punched him in the stomach. They started fighting as usual but we were always ready for that.

'Josh!' I yelled. I decided when we first started band to employ Josh as a bouncer and it only cost me a chocolate bar a week. We had to find some way of stopping Gaz or Charlie annoying or fighting people and we needed to give Josh a job. Still don't see why I paid him, he never did anything except start the fights.

'Yeah what?' he said, he looked like he had been disturbed doing something he shouldn't of. Then I noticed that Jade's shoe laces had been tied together and so had Del's. I pointed this out to them and then watched Jade slap Josh and Del try to kick him in the head but he couldn't reach and fell over.

By the time Josh finally came over to talk to me, Gaz and Charlie where trying to kill each other with chairs.

'Do you think you could do your job for once and split these two up?' I asked him politely otherwise he would moan.

'Do I have to? It's more fun watching them'

'I agree with you there but for the safety of the others in this room you might want to at least take them both outside. They can kill each other but not us'

'So I can still watch them kill each other outside?'

'I guess'

'Yay! I can even make the others pay to watch!'

'No you can't'

'Spoil sport!'

'That's my job' I replied as he carried Gaz and Charlie outside, I did say he was strong.

Chapter 7 - Lectures, Concerts and Old Friends

So the days dragged by leading up to the gig. I was getting really nervous, started think what if we messed up? What if there's another fight again? But then I remembered our security team which makes it even worse. There was Josh in charge which can only be a good thing, I mean he's so strong he beat our P.E teacher in an arm-wrestle. Then we had Andy who wasn't particularly strong (or smart for that matter) but he was useful just to look after the equipment. Then, for the big finale, we have (drum roll please) ... Del! The weediest person you'll ever meet in your life! It's quite funny actually because he tries to stop people getting to us and they just pick him up and put him aside.

The strain had started to show on everyone, Charlie (who played guitar with me) was ready to lash out at anyone anytime. Gaz was just really quiet and Christy couldn't even cheer him up. Jade was quite nervous but as usual only let me see that. Alex was more stressed than usual which is saying something. Jasmine was going completely bonkers trying to cheer everyone up and Louise was just as bad.

The final practice before was hectic but one of the best we had ever had. Gaz didn't miss a single beat, Jade reached every note, Alex stayed in rhythm and Charlie and I were in perfect synchronisation on the songs where there was only one part. I even managed to teach them the new song I wrote and they instantly got it, well I pride myself on making idiot proof songs, yet Charlie still managed to get some of them wrong... but then again that's Charlie... best not dwell on it or ill give myself another headache.

Then we all went home so we didn't have to try to hide our nervousness from the others, even though we didn't do a good job of hiding it when we were all together.

I decided not to have a practice on Friday because I thought we could all do with a bit of alone time with our nerves, you never know they might have found a way round them. But at four o'clock I left my house, because we planned to get there a couple of hours early in case we needed to set anything up, and headed for Gaz's house.

He was waiting outside his house and as soon as he saw us he ran for the car dodging things that seemed to be getting thrown at him from the upstairs of his house.

'Drive!' he said as soon as he was in the car.

'What the hell was that about?' I asked him after my mum gave me one of those strange looks that's says "is that normal?"

'Well you know about me and Christy?' I nodded 'Yeah well mum didn't and Christy phoned to find out where the place is and my mum answered it and well... she hates me not telling her stuff like that.' He finished looking embarrassed but relieved that he still had all his limbs intact. Note to self I thought as we went to get Charlie never get on the wrong side of Gaz's mum.

'Is Christy gunna be there?' my mum asked with another strange look in her eyes that kind of said "she must be really pretty for Gaz to risk his mum's wrath on"

'Yeah she's gunna get there not long after us and I think she's bringing Pete and Alida. You know what Alida and Christy are like, can't separate them for long and Christy's been with me all day.' He said. Yet again a perfect truth, Christy and Alida both started at our school at the same time and have been best friends since... well forever I think.

'Is anyone else from school going?' I asked, the nerves starting to kick in again.

'Yeah actually, pretty much everyone is going to be there. It's a big celebration night tonight and everything's half price I think.'

'What are they celebrating?'

'Some partially famous band having an anniversary party and they are supposed to play after us. I can't remember the band's name but I remember it's some sort of band girls go crazy over. Good night to have a girlfriend.'

I so wished he hadn't added that last bit while my mum was within earshot. Whenever something like that was said that could possibly suggest anything sexual my mum started lecturing me and now she was probably going to lecture Gaz as well. This was the second most embarrassing thing that had happened in my life at this point. The first... well let's say I was really drunk and was really glad I couldn't remember it if what my friends told me was true... makes me cringe just thinking about it...

I was really glad I could get out of the car to go get Charlie; actually I think Gaz was too because he got out as well.

I knocked on the door and yet again it wasn't Charlie who answered. But it wasn't Carl it was Sarah.

'Hey I'll just get Charlie' I looked at Gaz who also looked puzzled; I could swear I told Charlie to make sure Sarah could make her own way there...

'Hey' Charlie said as he appeared at the door followed by his mum dad, Carl and what looked like one of Sarah's friends.

I looked at him with a confused expression and counted all the people. 1, 2, 3, 4, 5 6, plus me plus Gaz plus mum plus John equals... 10!

'How big do you think our car is?' I asked him

'Oh no don't worry, they are just gunna follow in the other car. My dad doesn't actually know where he's going so... you know...'

'No I don't actually you can explain in the car, just don't say anything about girlfriends unless you want an earful from my mum' I finished still embarrassed and we got in the car.

We were going up the motorway; don't ask me why I'm no good at geography, in deep conversation so my mum couldn't interrupt us again.

'...well why didn't you turn up for the party round Gaz's at the weekend?' I was asking Charlie.

He turned around to indicate he was with Sarah and then looked back at me with a puzzled expression on his face. He looked back behind us and I followed his eyes to see a red Mondeo behind us.

'What you looking at?' I asked him

'Where are they?' he asked

I looked back and sure enough there was no sign of the black Volvo. Not behind the Mondeo, or the car behind that, or the car behind that, or anywhere.

'Mum... err... man overboard?'

'What are you on about?' she asked me

'Err we kind of... err... lost Charlie's lot' I said and we all looked at each other.

At the same time we all got out our mobiles, don't know what for though, I had no credit, Gaz's phone's speaker didn't work and Charlie was the only one with any of their numbers. At least we could say we had good intensions.

'Hello?' he said after a few seconds of the phone ringing 'where are you? Oh hey Mrs Duncan I take it Sarah left her mobile at home? Yeah I thought so; at least that explains why you answered the phone. Never mind I'll see you later Mrs Duncan, bye'

'Mrs Duncan?' I said sarcastically 'Why don't you call her ma'am there's a lot less to say that way.'

'Dunno what your laughing at you still call Jade's mum Mrs Barthel! Anyway now I've got to try calling my mum and that's never a… pleasant experience' he said and called his mum.

Turned out they had over taken us ages ago because my mum was driving too slowly. Luckily Sarah's friend knew where to go.

We got to the club without another incident apart from Charlie and Gaz trying to fight each other again. We got out of the car to find the others unpacking the instruments and typically Josh was carrying most of the drum kit at once.

I ran forward just in time and caught the guitar that Del had dropped and was about to smash in two on the floor.

'Good reactions' said Del 'you're here just in time because there are some people here who keep trying to take the stuff'

He pointed at a group of people at the side of the van. It was Charlie's mum and dad followed by Sarah and her friend.

'That's Charlie's family and girlfriend plus friend from school. They can help if they want to, Sarah's an old school friend, very trust worthy but not to strong so just give her some wires or something' Del laughed and I went to find the club manager.

The first thing that came into my head as I stepped inside was wow! It was huge! A very large stage at one end, disco lights covering the ceiling apart from one circle in the middle where there was a window so you could see the sky.

'This place is amazing!' Jade said as she walked up to me.

'Amazing isn't the word! It's incredible! It's… Filaffellum!' don't worry I'm not going crazy, well I already was but that's beside the point. Filaffellum is a word Jade made up… well ages ago and it supposedly means whatever you need it to. Useful when there are things you can't describe with words. Even though my philosophy is you can explain everything, except luck and love so you can't always use it. Anyway enough of my ramblings, back to the story.

We went up to Freddy McNeal's office to check everything is on schedule. We knocked on the door and got a very bright 'come in'

'Ah you've arrived, I'm Freddy McNeal but you can call me Freddy' he said shaking my hand.

'Good to finally meet you Freddy, this is my Girlfriend Jade' I said and Jade waved from behind me 'we just came up to check everything's on schedule.'

'Well it will be ready as soon as you give me your play list so I can put it on the leaflets.'

'Ah yes of course it's right-' I put my hand in my pocket and it wasn't there. I checked my coat pocket my back pocket and it wasn't there! It wasn't anywhere!

'Looking for this?' Jade said holding up a piece of paper headed play list in my handwriting.

'You're a life saver! I'll make it up to you later' I said

'Will you now? Hmm… that sounds interesting…' she said and I turned back to Freddy smiling.

'Here you go. Sorry if you can't read it my handwriting is terrible' I said a little embarrassed handing him the play list.

'Good, good, that's everything then,' we turned to walk out 'but can I have a private word Martin?'

I turned to look at Freddy then said 'sure' I turned to Jade 'I'll be down in a bit' and she walked out to go help the others. 'So what is it?'

'You do understand the risks of having a relationship with a fellow band member don't you? Because if you two split up it may cause the others to have to pick a side'

'I understand what you're saying but I've assessed the risks and if I had to I would leave the band as long as we could be together. Sir, she's well worth the risk. Let me ask you something, have you ever been in love?'

'Yes, once a long time ago'

'Well then you may be able to understand what I feel like when I'm with her. It's a feeling that I would give everything I have to hold on to and if it comes to it I will. I'll leave you with one last question, what lengths and risks would you go to have that feeling again?'

He sat down in his chair, nodded showing that he understood what I was saying and then I walked to the door. I pulled it open and Jade fell into the room.

'Oops! Busted!' she said laughing I helped her up and we walked down the corridor laughing all the way. 'Did you mean that?' she said when we were outside the receptionist's office.

'You know I'm sure you've asked me that before? And do you know what else? I'm sure it's the same answer'

'Umm… what was your answer last time?' she really was just as forgetful as I was and that's saying a lot!

I just carried on walking trying not to laugh while she tried to get me to tell her, but as you should know by now I'm really stubborn, she was just going to have to remember.

Well a few hours later we were back stage getting ready to go on, now that's the worst part of the whole thing because the nerves are completely built up and you know there's no way out of it anymore. Its fine when you're on stage and already performing but the bit before is terrible. Actually now I think of it this was the first time nobody threw up before we went on.

Well they announced us as "possibly the next big thing to hit Aldershot", which made everyone feel even worse, I'll have to tell them that it doesn't help when they pile on the pressure like that I thought. Then before I knew it we were all up on the stage playing the first song which was As Lovers Go by Dashboard Confessional, I had to put that one in there because it was mine and Jade's song.

There were a few slip ups while we were on stage, for instance I tripped up and fell on the floor but I managed to make it look like I was being an over enthusiastic guitarist.

It went really well actually compared to our past gigs even with the little slip ups.

We had to finish on a slow song so we played Heaven by DJ Sammy. Which was ok because I didn't have to do anything it was down to Keith and Jade but they did really, really well.

It was really good afterwards because we got to stay and listen to the partially famous band after us which we actually knew. It was Ben Hardiman, Steve Hickson (Norwegian Stevegon (don't ask me why we call Steve Norwegian Stevegon it's a long story)) and Luis something. Basically a band called Trampazy who me and Jade met when we went to Wales earlier that year, we all became really good friends in Wales and me and Ben were called the six foot three people even though I was about an inch taller than him (don't ask me how that works either).

Jade and I went backstage when they had finished, to see them and congratulate them.

'Martin! Jade! Saw you on stage, very nice!' said Ben as soon as he saw us. We were two of those bands who didn't let popularity or competition get in the way of being friends.

'You didn't do so bad yourself!' I said back to him after a manly hug, 'how you doing Ben?'

'Great!' Ben was a nutcase basically, when we were in Wales we had to do entertainment one night so we did impressions. Ben dressed up as a girl called Patsy from my school; he had the makeup, the pink jacket, the hair and even the bra which we had to stuff with Patsy's green hiking socks.

'Norwegian?'

'Same,' Norwegian was another Ben only more camp, 'you two?'

'We're good' said Jade 'What about you Luis?'

'I'm good, glad to see you two are ok' he said, Luis was the tough man but could also be funny at the same time.

'You know what? Funnily enough, so am I' I said we started walking towards the dance floor when I saw something I thought I'd never see. I showed Jade and she looked just as astonished as me. Coming of the dance floor was Del, lips locked with this dark haired girl; she was dragging him towards the toilet.

He saw us, gave us two thumbs up and then was gone. Jade and I looked at each other and then just burst out laughing.

The rest of the night was spent laughing, dancing and messing about. At half past one they had to start getting everyone out so the two bands went up to Freddy's office, Trampazy went up to say thank you as they weren't getting charged because they played. We however went up there so we could get paid. The fruits of our labour, a tenner each, brilliant considering all we took from them.

Chapter 8 - Instincts and Edd

Don't you just hate getting lost? Isn't it even worse when you get lost in a town you've lived in for however many years? Well me and Edd, well let's just say we get lost too often. Like back in the summer holidays before we started year ten.

We started, as usual when we go on random explorations of Bracknell and the surrounding area, by meeting at the back of his house with our bikes. Then we chose a random direction to go. After about twenty seconds of deliberating, it wasn't a hard choice it was either left or right, we started going down the road towards a big field where they were planning on building a new town but changed their mind and just started building a road instead.

When I was young a very wise old man, that just happened to be my granddad, told me "you should always follow your instincts and if they get you into trouble use your head to get you out of it" and in his memory I always have.

Now I should tell you that my instincts have never failed to get in me into trouble even if I do find something useful or something I could help with. Edd's instincts weren't much different from mine but they always said something different to mine. So for this reason we were quite surprised when they both said the same thing for once.

We were just riding past the woods where we did our archery when my instincts kicked in.

'Edd, my instincts again mate' I said skidding and turning to him

'Yeah mine too' he replied 'on three point to where they say we should go, one, two, three.'

We both pointed south west, the way the new road was heading. We looked at each other for a minute astounded that we agreed on something for once.

'Now that's a first!' I said to him still a little bit shocked 'now that tells me it's something important we're supposed to find or do. Either that or I'm reading too much into things again' I was, and still am, a strong believer in destiny and fate and stuff like that.

'normally I would say the latter but I'm not too sure...' he had that look on his face that with Edd means he's thinking, with other people it just means they're slightly constipated.

I looked at my watch, it was just past six and we had to be back before nine which meant we had loads of time to check it out.

'We still got just under three hours if we want to see what it is.' He didn't look convinced 'remember our promise to Granddad'

'I know it's just-'

'For once in your life do don't think, don't look before you leap and don't look both ways! Actually forget that last one I could do without having to drag you to hospital again' (long story short, Edd. Golf club. Edd's head. A lot of blood. Not a good combination.)

'Fine, fine just remember it's your fault if I get killed'

'Well everything else is my fault anyway, it's my fault Jade poked the teacher, my fault I was born. Hey you get used to it'

So we headed down the road. The first thing we found was a dirt track which the construction vehicles used. Then some makeshift jumps that Edd wouldn't let me have a go on (spoil sport) and then the road came onto an already existing road.

'Hey isn't that the place that Aaron got married?' I asked, Aaron was my brother, he had gotten married a week before the start of the story so I couldn't be bothered to write about it. Who knows maybe I'll have a recollection of it later if you're lucky, but I do have to say one thing about that day, damn Jade looked beautiful!

'Yeah I think it is, wanna go have a look down there?'

'Sure why not' so we headed down there, all the memories flooding back so fast I nearly went into a bush. 'I know this is childish but... race you back!'

'You're on!' Edd replied. But even with his freakishly long legs I still beat him, but that's not saying much.

We carried on the road we were on before we started going on the one we just raced on. And yes I did make that sentence to be confusing, if it didn't confuse you then give yourself a pat on the back. Well done!

Anyway we followed the road until it came alongside a field with lots of white fluffy things in it. They were-

'SHEEP!' I shouted at the top of my voice. Ever since I went to Wales I was always astounded that there were still enough sheep for the rest of the world.

I shouted so loud that the sheep ran away from us, the look of terror on what you could see of their faces! Ah satisfaction! (I know I'm the nice guy but being so nice I have to be evil in other parts of life to get rid of my evilness. There's method in the madness even if it is complete and utter tripe!)

'You know, for the amount of them they aren't too bright.' I said turning to Edd, 'I mean they are all running away from us yet not one of them has noticed there's a barbed wire fence in between them and us.'

'You know, even for you, what you just said was very random. True, but still random.'

'Hey I get it from Jade'

'Yeah, that's not a good thing mate'

'It is for me, life's a lot funnier when you're random and dirty minded. Anyway of course I'm random, you're talking to the person who was having lunch with Jade's family and thought it would be funny to see a drunken wasp. Still dunno what it would do, I mean would it fly into the wall? Would it fly into you a lot then say "what did you say about ma wife?"? Could it even fly? Would it be illegal? Or could they-'

'Yeah Martin... shut up'

'Fine! I will! No wait that's not what I'm supposed to say is it?' I asked confused

'Nope, but you said it now so you got to'

'Damn!'

'Anyway I told you they would drown and wouldn't be able to drink it'

'But how do you know?'

He sighed and said 'I just do. Anyway let's keep going, I doubt our instincts wanted us to see some sheep.'

'Del would. Oh yeah that's what I was supposed to tell you! Del's moving to America'

'Really, when?'

'Err when's the eighteenth?'

'Tomorrow'

'Right well he told me not to go to his house from the eighteenth onwards so that would mean he left... today! Wait... crap!'

'You're good'

'What is it with you and stating the painfully obvious?' I asked him but he didn't reply.

We carried on following the road, I nearly got hit by a car going past so we decided to pull over whenever a car came past. Stupid traffic...

We came to the end of the road, onto a roundabout. Now this place I knew, it was the roundabout on the nine mile ride at the end of old Wokingham road.

'Hey it'll be getting dark soon, you know how grandma gets about staying out after dark' I shouted to Edd over the noise of the traffic. Edd lived with our grandma instead of with his mum. This is because his mum worked shifts and had done since Edd was a baby, Beverly couldn't leave him on his own all day because Edd's dad didn't want to know. So he lived with grandma when he was little and just never left. He still kept in contact with his mum and step dad, Chris.

'We aren't going to make it back in time, we should head to my mums and ask whether Chris can give us a lift home' he shouted back to me.

'What about the bikes? Chris's car isn't big enough'

'We can leave them at my mums and get a lift back in the morning to take them home'

'But that means we have to do this all again!' I shouted outraged 'if I do this again I will end up throttling someone, and you'd be the closest' the whole thing was fun and everything but very tiring and stressful.

'Stop moaning 'n let's go, there's a storm coming' and true enough there was a very nasty looking black cloud coming at us.

So we went to the end of the nine mile ride to a double roundabout. By this time we were in the middle of a torrential down pour but here we encountered another problem. There was no more cycle path to get to Beverley's house.

'Why don't we just ride on the road?' Edd suggested

'One, this is a main road and you'd get hit by a car eventually. Two, the road is really slippery and you'd fall off and get run over by an eighteen wheeler. Three because it would be faster just to go back the way we came.'

'You really don't like riding on the roads do you' he shouted as a truck went past us.

'I don't mind riding on the road as long as the chances are I'll live to see Jade again. You know she'd bring me back from the dead just to kill me again for dying before her! I'd prefer to die just the once thanks.'

'Fairy snuff' he said laughing

'You've been hanging round Del too much'

'Yeah probably have. I think five minutes is too long actually'

Oh yeah just in case you couldn't figure out what Edd meant by fairy snuff, that's what Del always said instead of fair enough. Don't ask me why because I have absolutely no idea.

So we rode home but not before we had a not so interesting talk with a police officer about how we didn't have lights on our bikes, weren't wearing helmets and were wearing dark clothes. So we aren't exactly perfect, I'm the closest you're going to get to it! Actually that's a complete and utter lie but what you gunna do, sue me?

This is a note from the authors lawyer please do not sue my client or send any death threats. All resemblance to any character or copy righted object was not intentional.

Stupid lawyer!

Chapter 9 – Guitars and Geeks

Right so up to this point I haven't proven much of this "nice guy" status so I figured I should show you my volunteer work (well you can call it work anyway). First off you know I play guitar, if you don't then you were clearly not paying attention a few chapters ago or you have some sort of amnesia, either way you suck. But back to the point, I play guitar and have for a couple of years now, I taught myself to play with a little assistance from Edd (who btw is amazing at it which is really annoying since I technically started playing before he did but that's a whole other story) and I know it was bloody hard but I'm proud of myself for doing it. Anyway Linda wanted to learn how to play too so I started teaching her, once a week we'd go to our maths teacher Mr Jones and smile sweetly and ask if we can basically make a lot of noise and get in his way while I attempt to teach something I haven't learned properly.

So after a while Linda is at my level and I can't teach her anymore so she starts teaching herself too but that left me with a problem, I discovered (and this is hard for me to say as a teenager that has spent the majority of his life rebelling against teachers) I like teaching. So I found some more students but as it turned out there were more than I could teach so I roped Linda in to helping me.

'OK Splish, now play the A Major' I said for the umpteenth time. Splish was one of Jade's mate's sister's (and yes that is the easiest way I could put it), if she tried she could do really well but she was very easily distracted. One day she managed so much that we had time to invent a game (which involved balancing the guitar in the palm of your hand and timing it which accounted for many of the dents and scratches on my guitars. But Splish was on one of her off days today.

'I'm trying to remember!' she snapped, she's one of these girls that like to be on the offensive. 'Is this it?'

'No that's the E Minor, close though'

'How about this?' she said getting more and more frustrated.

'A Minor but your very close'

'Ok this has to be it' she strummed and I cringed as all the notes clashed together in nothing even resembling a chord this time. You know the nails down a chalk board thing right? This gets me worse than an orchestra of people running their nails down hundreds of chalk boards.

'Ok Splish what's up with you today?' I asked finally, I figured that after half an hour or not remembering one chord this might speed things up.

Immediately she put the guitar down (you can always tell when a girl need to say something because they jump at the first opportunity) and looked up at me sitting on the table, she was a year below me and a girl so obviously I could only be so much help but I had to try. 'So this morning yeah, I was talking to Dillon about stuff... well mostly about nothing but we never really talk about anything in particular you know?' I nodded whilst internally shaking my head (she was a girl, she didn't have to make sense), 'And then all of a sudden he says "this isn't working out" and dumps me!"

Ok this was now difficult because part of me wanted to laugh at her impression of Dillon (which was awful) and the other part realised that this girl really needed a hug which came up with two problems. Firstly before you say anything it has nothing to do with being a man and not being able to show feelings or any crap like that, a real man has no problem showing some emotion. The first problem was that I'm her teacher; don't get me wrong she was very attractive but one I love Jade and two her mum (who worked in the student reception) had already given me one of those "don't you dare" looks when I agreed to teach her daughter. Now I know that giving a girl a hug doesn't mean we're gunna get married or anything but I also know that young girls fall for guys way too easily.

The second problem was that Splish wasn't a normal girl, she may have cute nickname (her real name obviously isn't Splish its Ashley which was changed to Splash when she took up swimming but turned to Splish Splash and now just Splish, I know it's weird but what nickname sounds normal when you have to explain it?) but I swear she could breathe fire if she wanted to, you've never seen a temper like hers, she could outmatch me probably. I'm sure you know someone like her, the one that always has to have the last word in any argument and makes sure she does by slamming a door behind her.

So all in all, a hug wasn't the best plan. She carried on fuming and venting until she was all vented out, by the end of it I was no closer to knowing what happened between them but she seemed to feel better about it so hey.

Linda was in the other room with Rose teaching her to do power chords; I could hear them playing songs by mine and Linda's favourite band. Linda taught the more advance class so I could help those having trouble which was just Splish today since Nathan was ill. Since it was just us two I could get away with helping her a little bit.

'I've got an idea; do you think you could distract Mr Jones for a few minutes?'

She looked at me puzzled for a moment before asking 'How am I supposed to do that? And why would I want to?'

'Do you want revenge on Dillon?' she nodded after a moment, 'then distract him and I'll take care of the rest.'

'Ok but how am I supposed to do that?' she asked glancing over at the Canadian teacher with thinning hair. I liked Mr Jones because he was some sort of uber geek and didn't take it too hard on the students, in fact he could barely keep control of them but it made me feel sorry for him.

'Simple, ask him to explain about all the rings in the Lord of the Rings. Oh and try to look interested in the answer.'

'Is that really gunna work?' she asked looking between him and me in bewilderment.

'Mr Jones!' I called over the class room and the sounds of guitars

'Yes Martin?' he asked without looking away from his computer screen

'Can you come here a sec? Ashley has a question for you,' I said smirking at her.

'If it's anything Maths related can it wait for class?'

'Oh no sir, its nothing like that, it's about one of your favourite subjects.' Now he turned to me looking curious.

'Which subject is that?'

'LOTR' I used the abbreviation as a real geek would, typically that got him straight out of his chair and over to us.

When asked Mr Jones went into a really passionate and detailed description/ explanation of the background of the Lord of the Rings. He had spent the entirety of one of our hour and a half guitar lessons doing an impossible LOTR quiz online before. I'm sure you'd be really surprised to hear he ran a fantasy war game club too.

Anyway while he was being the geekiest person alive I was sneaking onto his computer and using his teacher security levels on the network to access Dillon's files and download some… incriminating files to his desktop, the next time he logged on his background would be covered in pictures of actors that girls drooled over.

Anyway a week later she was back together with Dillon so my genius was once again wasted. Women.

Chapter 10 - In The End, I Went Out Smiling

Well here it is... the bit the story has been leading to. This is the final chapter of this story, the big finale, the... some other way of saying the end that's really cheesy and over used.

Everything seemed normal when I woke up, jumped down the stairs... nearly broke my ankle... hit my head on the way into the shed where I keep my bike.

I was on my way to meet up with the guys. We were having a guys day out, no pressure from girls, no worrying about anything, no frowns... well apart from the adults giving us strange looks but they don't count. The original plan was to go paintballing but we weren't organised enough to book it so we went bowling instead since in Bracknell the social decisions are quite limited if you don't want to mug old grannies like the majority of the population seemed to.

'Hey!' I yelled to the group already waiting for me outside the bowling alley. It was a big collection of guys this time; Charlie, Gaz, Keith, Josh, Carl, Rodney (good mate but not exactly... athletic), Jamie, Bruce (one of my best friends since year eight), Nick (a Polish guy who came to our school in year nine and I was the only one who could work out what he was saying at first so he hung around with me until his English got better), Will, Andy, Alex (from the archery chapter), Edd and Ben. That makes... twelve... carry the four... divide by pie... fifteen of us all together. Should be fun... all I can say is that I was glad I was not paying for everyone.

So we got in and instantly Edd had a problem. There were no bowling shoes his size left and he couldn't wear his trainers. You could almost imagine the giant orange orang-utan/ clown convention in the corner having a game and tripping over constantly, I mean how else could they possible run out of size fourteens?! Luckily, for him I persuaded them to let him play without shoes on, seemed like a good idea until the smell hits you. The things you do for family.

So we played the first round and three people got strikes. Next round the same, three got strikes. And the next round, and the next. I could feel my chances of victory ebbing away.

Halfway through our second game (I came eleventh in the last game but I was in third this time) I was taking my shot, it started curling to the left, then it went in the gutter. I turned around and found myself face to face with Jade. I recoiled with the shock and fell flat on my ass (yes I did land flat on a donkey).

'I hope you haven't been playing like that all through the game' She said mockingly.

Holding her close to me I said 'No of course not! I've been hammering these guys! They think of me as a bowling god you see-' at that moment I had a load of empty cups and jackets thrown at me... and even a shoe.

'Somehow I don't think they agree,' Jade said laughing 'when are you finished?' she said with an evil, sexy note in her voice and the note turned to a look in her eye.

'As soon as you want me to be,' I said being the loving boyfriend I'm known to be 'What are you doing here anyway?'

'I was shopping with the girls then I remembered you said you'd be here so I thought I'd take you back to my house for a couple of hours.' She said with that look in her eyes still.

I jumped at the idea and turned to ask the guys if someone would take my goes for me. Then I saw that they were looking from me to Jade with their mouth gaping. Charlie wolf whistled and then everyone else started telling me to have "fun". Men! Come on girls you know what I'm talking about! Wait... I'm a man too... sorry guys.

'I hope you know that you've just pushed my reputation right up!' I said to her once we were outside.

'Well it couldn't have done it any damage.'

'I love you, you know that' I whispered in her ear as we were coming up to a crossing going over the main road

'I love you too' she replied and I did my joking celebration dance.

Here is where it all went wrong. I lost my balance and stumbled into the middle of the road. I remember seeing a pair of headlights from one of those coupe/ sports cars. It struck my legs and sent me flying. I remember seeing the look of terror on Jade's face as I flew through the air. I didn't make any noise so as not to make it worse for her. I landed head first in the middle of the road.

I opened my eyes a moment later to see a pair of watery, bluey- green eyes looking at me. The eyes I knew so well. It made me smile. I didn't have the strength to talk. My neck and skull had been fractured in multiple places. There was no hope for me. I just reached out and brushed my bloody hand gently against her face. I'm glad that the last thing I saw was those beautiful eyes.

I died there and then. No more joking around with my friends. No more parties with my family. No seeing John grow up. No family of my own. I'll never again get to see Jade's smile. I'll never get that warm, safe feeling from just being with her.

Life is for living so make the most of what you have. There is always someone who loves, who will miss you, who will morn you when you are gone. Never give up and do not let insecurities or inhibitions get in the way of who you're supposed to be.

Epilogue

Well now I'm here, I don't quite know where here is but it doesn't hurt. Actually I don't feel anything which is even stranger, all I can see is white, like one of those cheesy movies where a guy has an "out of body experience" and just floats or walks around doing nothing. I dunno where I am but they need to call one of those DIY shows for a make-over. There's a whisper in the air that I can't quite make out, like someone talking at you from fifty feet away as if you were right next to them.

'Martin?'

Ok this either means I'm way too self-centred or someone else is here, hopefully not the creepy murderer in a mask kind of someone else either...

Beep... Beep

That's definitely not my phone either

'Quick get someone! I think he's coming around!'

The voice was louder now, a familiar voice, a voice I knew so well, almost better than my own. As the voice grew louder I started to consider if I was going crazy, you know that whole voices in your head not being a good sign and everything. Then feeling stared coming back too, I was laying down, my muscles were really weak and.... I was damn hungry.

Beep...Beep

Someone really needs to find their charger, that phone does not sound happy.

'Look he's moving his hands! His eyes are moving!'

Hang on a second, the last thing I remember is being hit by a car and dying, if they're talking about me then I'm either a zombie or Jesus mark two.

'Martin can you hear us?'

Of course I can hear you, you're shouting at me! Christ it's not like I'm deaf!

"Martin, open your eyes!'

So I did, my eyes were blinded instantly. As they slowly adjusted I could see more of what was around me. The silhouettes of people's heads, the polystyrene ceiling tiles broken up only by halogen lights.

There were three people around me, a woman and two men. One of the men was directly over me with a stethoscope in his ears, his short grey hair and wrinkled face were all business, no emotion on his face, this doctor was at work. I hate doctors ok, that's my excuse. With a very dry throat I croaked out five words 'Get the hell off me!' I tried to shove him off me but my arms were so heavy the best I could do was to wave his arms away but even that exhausted me.

'Haha still the good old Martin,' the other man said, I could hardly believe it, it was my brother Aaron but it wasn't... he was older; his hair line had receded further than I remembered, and his hair was also thinner and greyer. I looked at the woman but my mum looked just the same, maybe a little greyer too and a little thinner.

'Martin!' she cried and hugged me, now I had absolutely no clue what was happening, this was only the second time I'd seen mum cry, the first being when my granddad died and now this, what the hell was she crying about anyway?

'Does someone wanna tell me what's going on? What the hell happened to you guys? And I really need a drink.' I croaked out weakly.

'What do you remember?' Aaron asked me grabbing a tiny square from his pocket and running his fingers over it and tapping it frantically.

'Err... dying I think... is Jade ok? What happened?'

'Martin you've been in a coma for six years,' The doctor explained to me, it sounded like some bad joke at first but then it started slotting into place with everything else, why my arms were so weak, why they were older, why mum was crying, why I was so weak (obviously there was no keep fit program for coma patients). Apparently jade had called an ambulance and had stayed with me for three days straight until I was stable. At first she was at my bedside as often as she could be but she came less and less as the years went on. Three years ago she told my mum she couldn't spend her life waiting anymore; she was in her second year of college and couldn't keep it all up. In short she gave up on me but I couldn't blame her for that could I? Promises of being together forever ran through my head over and over again.

I spent the next couple of weeks in the hospital, doing physiotherapy and other tests, doing counselling sessions and seeing every member of my family including some new additions I didn't know. My brother was married again, my new sister in law Helena had a son from a previous relationship but he was no less my nephew now, they also had a daughter together called Mia who was one years old and just walking. My sister also had a little girl called Taliya who was nine months old; I had two new cousins and a new uncle. I had also lost my cousin Becca to cancer which hit me hard.

It was like being thrust into someone else's life, or reading the first book in a series and then skipping to the last and trying to understand what was going on. Six years is a long time, take a look at your life now and what it was like six years ago and you'll have an idea of what I was going through. I was confused, so happy and sad at the same time.

I had so much to catch up on, the world in general, people's lives, even technology. Apparently mobile phones didn't need buttons anymore which is cool but strange to me at the same time, my games console is now seriously out of date and super cars now top 200mph.

'I've sent out invites to people for you birthday party on Saturday, I invited all your old friends but don't be disappointed if only a few turn up, most are in university now remember.' My sister was setting up a birthday party for me and using it as a reason to bombard me with more people and things I need to work out and catch up with.

'Hang on, how can you contact all my friends? You never had their phone numbers and even if you did they would have changed by now surely?'

'No we made a Facebook group for you so we could keep people updated on your condition easier'

'Hang on, a what book?'

'Facebook'

'Which is?'

'Oh it's a social networking site,' I just looked at her completely bewildered with no idea what she was talking about. 'It's a website where people write things about themselves and all the people on their friends list can see and comment on it, you can also play games and make events to invite people to.'

'Ok so it's like being able to have a conversation with lots of people just over the internet and then they added some other stuff to keep you entertained so you don't realise that's a rubbish idea?'

'Basically yeah'

'ok…' so Saturday came way too soon, I was so nervous, I mean I'd seen most of my family by this point but now I was gunna see my friends who had officially left puberty and my knowledge of them behind. Most people couldn't turn up like my sister said but the few who did were completely different, it was kind of awkward. In my head this is my fifteenth birthday party, in reality it was my twenty first, apparently a lot changes in that time, changes I hadn't gone through yet.

Then it got really awkward. The doorbell went so I answered it not knowing who to expect this time, and I saw those bluey-green eyes again for the first time in six years even though to me it was only a few weeks. Jade Barthel stood at my door, my (it still felt weird to say it) ex-girlfriend.

'Happy Birthday Martin' she said uncomfortably holding out a card, 'I'm sorry I can't stay, I wasn't going to come at all, I didn't know how you felt about it all, it must be hard. I just want to say I'm sorry things turned out this way.'

She turned to walk away but I grabbed her hand instinctively and felt something hard and pointy pressing into my palm. She stopped and I looked at the ring on her finger. In shock I let her hand go, 'You're engaged?'

'I'm sorry Martin,' she said her eyes watery again as she walked away.

I stood there stunned for a moment before gathering myself together, she was engaged, so what? That didn't change my decision. I ran after her, she stopped when I called her name but she didn't turn to look at me.

'Jade wait,' I didn't know exactly how to say it, I'd been thinking about this moment for the past couple weeks and I'd decided what to do, now I just had to tell her. 'Jade I forgive you.'

She turned to look at me with a smile on her face, tears in her eyes 'Really?'

'Yes, I've thought about it and although it seems like we should still be together to me it hasn't been like that to you for over three years. I can't blame you for anything because you stuck around longer than any other girl would have. I think you deserve a medal for being loyal as long as you did. I can't imagine how hard it must have been for you, and thank you for trying but you deserved to move on, to be happy, I don't blame you. There's not really anything to forgive. We both know that I still love you but because of that I have to let you go, I don't wanna make things harder for you.' I paused for a moment looking at the ground, this next bit was a little hard 'I'm happy you made a life for yourself and I'm happy you found someone you can love and looking at the size of that ring really loves you back.'

We both smiled at each other then we hugged a much needed hug and she kissed me on the cheek before driving off. That's what loving someone is, it's the ability to make sacrifices for them, to make them happy even if you're not.

So now I spend my life trying to fit in and get along with everything, trying to find my purpose in life, just like everyone else in the world. Nobody is totally in sync with what's around them, everybody feels like there should be something more. That's why when you fall in love you hold on to it so tightly, because at least you feel in sync with the other person.

Everyone has their own story, this was mine.

Zeitfracht Medien GmbH
Ferdinand-Jühlke-Straße 7
99095 Erfurt, Deutschland
produktsicherheit@kolibri360.de

Druck:
CPI Druckdienstleistungen GmbH
im Auftrag der
Zeitfracht Medien GmbH
Ein Unternehmen der Zeitfracht - Gruppe
Ferdinand-Jühlke-Str. 7
99095 Erfurt